# MARRIED TO A CHICAGO BULLY 2

FATIMA MUNROE

# ONE

**F**ree

"Is he dead?" I asked the nurse on duty.

"We cannot give out that information over the phone," she stressed painstakingly. "All I can say is—"

"Fuck what you 'can' say! I ASKED IF HE'S DEAD!"

"Ma'am, calm—"

"DON'T TELL ME TO CALM DOWN!" I slammed the phone down on the glass coffee table, creating a tiny crack. "Somebody come throw this shit away!"

My personal assistant ran in the room and began dragging the table out. "Free, I'm—"

"Don't fuck up my carpet! Pick that shit up!"

"Eddie! Vigo!" she yelled before clapping twice. Entering the room quickly, Nuritsa gave her command in their native language. They hurriedly picked up the table and carried it to the trash.

"Go to the hospital." I rubbed the headache that began at the base of my skull and was beginning to radiate outwards. "See if Atif Hermes is still alive, call me as soon as you know."

"Yes, Fr..."

"As SOON as you know!" I screamed, which did nothing for my headache. "Go. NOW!"

Nuritsa scurried out of the living room where I sat looking over the tree tops of the city of Milwaukee from the south end. I hated Wisconsin. It was always cold here. The snow, the wind, the rain...I was all set to go back to my beautiful, spacious estate in Simi Valley where it was dry, warm, and I didn't have to worry about snow, rain, or none of this Midwest nonsense. Before I left, I had to know about Atif Hermes.

"Atif." My silk robe rustled quietly as I stood up and walked to the window, palming the pane as my breath fogged the glass. It hurt me deeply that he didn't remember who I was, but that would all be rectified in time...

# TWO

K apri
"PRINCE! IS THAT ATIF!"

"Kapri, man, I don't know, for real. We just gotta wait until the doctors come back and tell us something," he stood nervously and watched the door.

*Please let him pull through this. Please,* I pleaded with whoever listened to prayers and hoped they heard mine. *I need him. My brothers need him. We need him. Please let him pull through...*

We watched the door to the I.C.U. as it opened slowly. The nurse removed her face mask and crept timidly towards us. "Are you here for Atif Hermes?" she questioned cautiously.

"Yes, we are," a voice came up behind us, resting her hand on my shoulder. "What is his condition, please?"

"Uhm, excuse me," Tanji asked the woman hanging on my arm, "who are you?"

"Oh, I'm Atif's aunt Nuritsa from the old country. I came as soon as I heard," she rushed.

"Nurse, please. Is he going to make it?" I begged. Tanji and Atif's aunt could finish their conversation on their own time. I needed to know if my love was going to live or not.

"The swelling of his brain is slowly going down, and the doctor is running tests on him now. He did say that your husband may suffer from some memory loss, however he cannot tell whether it'll be temporary or permanent. As soon as we know something more concrete, we'll let you know, Mrs. Hermes."

"So, he's still alive?" I questioned as Atif's aunt tightened her grip on my shoulder. I brushed her hand off of me so I could focus on what the nurse was saying.

"Yes, yes, he's still alive," she nodded. "We had another patient just brought in who went into cardiac arrest. You can stay if you want, Mrs. Hermes, but the rest of the family will have to leave in about twenty minutes," she advised before heading back in the I.C.U.

Breathing a sigh of relief, I turned to see Tanji staring heatedly at Atif's aunt, who had her eyes trained on my back. "Hello. Nuritsa, right?"

"Right," she spoke curtly. "So, you're my niece, I'm assuming? How long have you and Atif been married?"

"Hmph. No 'Hi, how you doing', or 'Welcome to the family'. Just getting straight down to business, huh?" Tanji kissed her teeth as she side eyed Atif's aunt. "Guess all y'all from the 'old country' rude as fuck."

"TANJI! Don't talk to Atif's aunt like that!" I yelled as Prince turned his back to us with his phone glued to his ear.

"I'm saying though. It's damn convenient of her to pop up out the blue when Atif go to the hospital in Milwaukee where he was up here taking care of some business," Tanji instigated.

"My sister called and told me to come," she explained.

"Atif's parents ain't here. Your sister who?" Prince questioned, standing at her side so he was speaking directly in her ear.

"My—my uhm—" she stuttered, fumbling with the straps on her Vuitton bag.

He whispered in her ear and she stood stone faced listening to his words. I could only imagine what he was saying to her judging from his facial expression. "Atif's aunt gotta go," he spoke to us through gritted teeth, still in her ear.

"This isn't over!" she grimaced in Prince's direction, turning to walk towards the elevators.

"I love it," I walked behind her as she headed to the elevator, rolling up my sleeves. "Keep that same energy when I cave yo' fucking face in!" Prince grabbed me before I could wrap my hand around her throat, because the way I was feeling, I was ready to kill this bitch. I lunged for her just as the elevator doors opened. Scurrying between the sliding doors, the elevator caught the bottom of her dress as it moved downwards. I hoped that shit ripped off and she walked out with her little flat ass pancaked to her back. "Who the fuck was that?"

"I don't know exactly who she was, but I know for a fact that Atif doesn't have an aunt. His father has a brother who passed away, and his mother was an only child, too," he rubbed his beard thoughtfully.

"My baby can't be here." I began pacing the tiled floor in the waiting room. "He can't be in this hospital, Prince! What am I gonna do without him? Huh? PRINCE!"

"Calm down, sis." Tanji rushed to where I stood, borderline hysterical. "He wouldn't want you upset, pregnant or not. You have to be strong for Atif."

*Be strong for Atif,* I thought, taking a seat in the nearest chair. I focused on those words...took comfort in those words. I had to be strong for Atif. My baby was fighting for his life, and it was important that I was strong for Atif. Any time I thought about him, it reminded me of his current situation, and that wasn't me being his strength. I had to focus on the good times. The day he treated me to a full body massage at the Ritz-Carlton. The day he surprised me and flew me to the Kentucky Derby. How his surprises in general were always so thoughtful, so sweet. I had to be strong for Atif.

"Thank you, Tanji. I do need to be strong for Atif." I took a deep breath in and directed my thoughts to those double doors down the hallway at the beautiful man in that bed who loved me sometimes more than I loved myself. I thought about the day he kicked Tanji's door in because I had him on do not disturb. I thought about the day he took me to Prince's mother's house to introduce me to my brothers when I thought he had kids. I thought about the night he told me about my brothers' therapy session and God wasn't pleased so he kicked my mother off of a pier and watched her drown. Atif was my everything. I needed him for my peace and my sanity. He HAD to pull through.

"Sis, we'll get Atif moved in twenty-four hours. You right, he don't need to be here," Prince reassured my aching soul. It pained me not being within his airspace; I took comfort knowing he was coming home when we were apart.

"Find out who that woman was, Prince. I got some words for her."

"Like what, sis? 'Tif ain't gonna like—"

"Don't worry about what 'Tif gonna like, let me worry about that. Get me that information." I stood up and went to the area where the nurse said I could sleep.

Growing up on Chicago's west side and being around him these past few months, I knew exactly how to handle this situation. Whoever the bitch was that came up here was first on my list, and next was this chick Free whose name seemed to be on Atif's lips every time he opened his mouth lately. As long as this woman was still drawing breath in her body, she was living on borrowed time.

# THREE

# TANJI

I felt sorry for Kapri. Every time she got her a piece of happiness, somebody came along and snatched it away. Now she had to deal with the stress of being pregnant, her fiancé in the hospital, and the situation with her little brothers. I was praying that she found some peace in her spirit.

So, we up here at the hospital, right? Minding our business. Look up and it's a woman leaning on Kapri like she knows us. I'm curious, so I ask her who she is. Why this woman say she Atif's auntie? I'm looking at her, and she looks NOTHING like this man. I mean, yeah, I know he's part Armenian, but hell all the Kardashians look alike and they part Armenian too. With Kapri focused on whether or not Atif was gonna make it, it was up to me to get some answers around here.

"You think Kapri gonna be okay up here alone?" I asked Prince as we walked hand in hand to the parking deck.

"You think we gonna be able to get Kapri to leave with us?" he shot back. "She'll be aight. I called some shooters up here to be with her. They on her floor now."

"Since it's just us," I began, waiting for him to open the passenger's side door to my car for me, "who was that woman?"

"She work for Free," he responded, climbing in on the driver's side. "Her personal assistant or some shit."

My eyebrow raised on its own; was this woman serious? "Free can't be that bold, can she?"

"Free a dub. Fuck that bitch," he grumbled, starting up the car and pulling out of the parking garage. "We got other shit to worry about."

Hearing his phone beep, I tuned him out; I figured his phone conversations from now on would be about the streets with Atif in the hospital. My phone vibrated in my back pocket while we rode down I-94, headed back to the city. Glancing over at Prince, who was frowning as he yelled at whoever, I disconnected the handset from the Bluetooth in my car and put my ear to the phone's speaker. "Hello."

"My mama wanna know what you gonna do with the kids," Monica, Steve's sister, hissed in my ear. "She said that since Steve gone, you shouldn't be dropping them off over here while you run the streets."

"Those her grandkids though. Ain't like I'm dropping off somebody else's kids, they related to y'all," I grumbled.

"Steve said Jenesis ain't his, and his fiancée don't feel comfortable..."

"HIS FIANCÈE? You do know Steve and I are still married right?"

"I know Tanji..."

"Put yo' mama on the phone. I want her to tell me this herself!" I yelled. Monica loved my kids, whether Steve claimed them or not. I didn't want to put her in a position to choose sides between me and that old bitch. His mother ain't never liked me, even after I birthed her first grandchild.

"Yeah," Steve's mother spoke snidely in the phone's speaker.

"So, my kids can't come to your house no more?"

"Naw, I don't want them lil' ragamuffins at my house!" she yelled. "My son said he was leavin' you when he died, and I'm glad he was!"

"Listen, you stupid bitch," I grumbled through gritted teeth, "I don't give a fuck about you or yo' muthafuckin' son! That nigga dead! You touch one hair on either of my babies' heads before I get there and..."

"And what, Tanji! You gonna kill me too?" she yelled.

"What the fuck are you talking about? I ain't never killed nobody in my life!"

"I know you killed my son! And my daughter-in-law is my witness that you jus' admitted to it!" she screamed crazily. "I'ma have yo' ass arrested, Tanji! Wait 'til the police hear this shit!"

"YOU GOT THAT BITCH AROUND MY KIDS? I'LL..."

Prince snatched the phone from my hand and ended the call. "Steve mama trying to set you up, baby. Don't let that old bitch bait you like that."

"Thank you, love." My heart was racing. The thumping in my head was deafening as my hands shook. Mentally I was counting backwards from 50 in order to calm myself down from this woman's words. She really thought I killed Steve and burned my own damn house down? What would've been my motivation, because I would've come out of the divorce looking lovely. And I didn't know about the insurance policy until Lieutenant Wiggins, Corporal Wiggins, Colonel Sanders called me. For real, what did I have to gain? Steve meant more to me alive than he did dead. At least with him alive I could've slapped some sense in his head. "Prince, I have something to tell you."

"What's that, sexy?"

I told him about Steve's commanding officer calling me and his 'fiancée'.

"Oh, I already knew about that."

"You knew? How you know?"

"God told me. Wait, Atif told me," he chuckled. "I was just waiting to see if you knew and if you'd say something."

"How long have you known?" Now I was looking at him crazy.

"Atif told me about it when we rode up here. He know shit on all y'all."

"Hmph. Fuck yo' friend too, Prince." I pouted, folding my arms across my chest.

He stopped the car in the middle of the expressway, turning to me. "First of all, that's my brother. Second, say that shit again and you'll be walking back to Chicago!"

"PRINCE! IT'S A FUCKING TRUCK..."

"I AIN'T FUCKIN' WIT'CHU, TANJI!"

"OKAY, OKAY!" I begged as the 18-wheeler sped towards us with the horn blaring. "PRINCE, I'M SORRY!"

"Aight then." He slammed his foot on the gas and we swerved out of the lane in just enough time to not be split into pieces. "Leave Atif out of whatever we got going on."

*See, this why I need me a military man or something. These street niggas be taking this brotherhood of theirs a little too far.*

FOUR

# PRINCE

Tanji was quiet for the rest of the ride, and I took the opportunity to think. She was letting Steve's mother talk cash money shit to her like she didn't have the upper hand in their little situation. After picking up Steve Jr. and my princess, I made sure Tanji and the kids got settled at my condo before heading out to hit the streets. These next few days would be stressful to a lesser nigga. Hmph. Y'all know I ain't a lesser nigga though. Of course I had to cancel the Miami trip. Hell, that was the last thing I needed to get done as far as I was concerned. First and foremost was finding Free and tying her up in somebody's basement until Atif gave the word on what he wanted done. I would've just shot the hoe, until I listened to the message on my phone.

When Atif walked in the house with Eisha, he called me while I was on the phone with Tanji. Somewhere between me not answering and him walking out that house, he got my voicemail. I don't know if he was trying to record their conversation or if he just forgot to hang up. However, it did give us some insight on why we hadn't rode up here before now to take care of Free. As much as he talked about putting hands around Free's throat, that was something that could've happened long before now if he really wanted her dead. He had no problem kicking Kapri's mother off that pier.

And as far as Eisha went, I agreed with Michaela; I couldn't believe I called that smut my girl at one point. Atif had to have known about Free and Eisha being related; they had those familial traits. Eisha was no better than the pack of wolves she sprung from—conniving, trifling, and shady as fuck. And if what she said on that recording was true, then I did right putting those two bullets in her neck.

Michaela, Michaela, Michaela...Damn. I wondered what was going on in her head that was so devastating; so dire that she felt the need to hang herself. I racked my brain going over the last time I saw her and her overall mood. My last memory of her was when Atif told me he'd catch up with me later. He never told me what they discussed, but I had my own suspicions. Right before he met Kapri, they all of a sudden became real close. Even those first few weeks when 'Tif and his girl were getting to know each other, Michaela seemed a little off. Not way out in left field, except for the fact that she wasn't her normal self either. She always wanted to know if I knew where he was if she couldn't get him on the phone. We knew when to bother Atif and when to leave that man alone, for some odd reason she made it seem like she had to know his every move.

Pulling up the video sent to me of Free's former mansion in Menomonee Falls, I smirked at the pile of rubble that my team was responsible for as the fire department searched for the hot spots still smoldering as the sun finished setting in the distance. I couldn't believe that her personal assistant was bold enough to pop up at the hospital trying to find out information on Atif. Kapri wasn't gonna like this shit, however it wasn't my place to get in the middle of what her fiancé had gotten himself into. Just like Atif didn't insert himself in my personal life, I showed him that same respect. Men don't concern themselves with other men's relationships anyway, that's a female trait.

Riding around the city, I checked the traps and made the pickups. With the majority of the team being out of town taking care of this little business with the God, I had to make sure these niggas stayed on task. Soon as I parked my car in the alley, my phone rang. One quick glance at the screen had me swiping right, putting my game face on. "What's good, my G?"

"Aye, you talked to the God?"

"He out of town, why?"

Jeff took a deep breath in and blew it out before speaking. "I need you to come out here to 73$^{rd}$ and Exchange."

"Say less." I hung up the phone, turning my truck to head to the south side. *If it ain't one thing, it's a muthafuckin' other,* I thought, sitting in traffic in the middle lane of the express lane on the Dan Ryan.

---

"GUESS WHAT I FOUND OUT?" Jeff smacked on a bag of chips as we stood outside the corner store and politicked, watching two zombies as they stumbled by.

"What."

"Michaela didn't commit suicide."

"Wait, ain't you the one that called me and said..."

"I saw her hanging with my own two eyes," he explained. "I'm telling you what I found out from some niggas up in the Mil."

"What you find out?"

"Some chick named Keisha, Meesha..."

"Eisha?"

"Yea, Eisha. Her and Eisha was beefed..."

I stopped and waited as he served a fiend, watching the block as he handled his business. "Where you said you heard this from?"

"Ol' girl who stayed downstairs said she heard arguing, then something loud hit the floor. She heard a lot of banging and chairs scraping before a bunch of muthafuckas ran down the back steps," he expressed.

"I'm trying to figure out what Michaela and Eisha was beefed about though," I looked down the block and watched twelve creeping up the street. "Who told you that up in Milwaukee?"

"I know this one chick…"

"Aye, unless you 'bout to tell me your girl got a girlfriend, I don't wanna hear no yatta-yatta between these females." I stopped him before he started.

"Nah, she know one of the niggas that was there that day. They broke in Kayla's crib and was there when she got home. Apparently, she was asking the wrong questions and Eisha didn't want nobody to find out, but by the time she got to her, Kayla already told the God."

"Oh, she ain't want nobody to know she was out here plotting up on the family? Man, fuck that bitch," I grumbled. "Fuck she think Kayla was gonna do, blackmail her stupid ass?"

Jeff shook his head, still smashing the bag of plain Lays. "Aye, I'on know. That's what I heard though."

"Aight, I'll get with the God and let him know. Tighten this shit up out here, y'all got the blocks too hot. Hit my line if anything else come up."

"No doubt," he dapped me up and we went our separate ways.

# FIVE

## ATIF

Watching her take slow, deliberate steps through the white sandy beach at the edge of the ocean, I cracked a small smile thinking of what was to come. Here was my bride, the woman I was going to spend the rest of my life with and I couldn't be happier. Pop stood next to me nodding his head up and down, his eyes crinkled into acceptance as I nervously anticipated our wedding night. Ma stood off to the side of me and I couldn't read her expression, but that wasn't my focus anyway. What I was focused on was getting those hips that were now swaying back and forth in the fleeting sunset stationary in the air as I slipped deeper and deeper between her thighs.

Her chest heaved slowly once her ascent to our wedded altar came to an end. The dress perfectly hugging her curves. I wanted to rip her clothes from her body on the spot, sliding my tongue between her plump lips as her eyes held the sparkle reserved for me and me alone. Glancing quickly at the officiant as he nodded for me to lift her wedding veil, I pinched both corners between my thumbs, lifting the delicate lace up to reveal her big brown orbs.

"Atif, I love you so much," Free spoke, smiling gently in my direction.

*Free?*

*FREE!*

*I reached back and punched her dead in her shit, blood spurting all over her lace dress as she stared at me with her gaped smirk.*

*"Atif, you love me! You know you love me, dammit! ATIIIFFF!"*

*"Get the fuck away from me, Free! I told you what the fuck was gonna happen if I ever saw your ass again!"*

*"Yet, you didn't, did you?" she screamed crazily, with blood and spittle dripping from her bottom lip. "You and Prince came up here and you let me live, Atif! WHY? BECAUSE YOU LOVE ME!" she yelled before hocking up a tooth.*

*"Look, bitch, I didn't spare your life because I fuckin' love you! I spared your life because..."*

*"Atif? You love her?" Kapri's voice came from behind me on my left side. I turned to see her and the boys looking at me with nothing but regret, making me feel like the biggest asshole in the world.*

*"Baby, let me explain..."*

*"Atif, how could you? How could you do that to me?" She began crying as her little brother Jacari turned to console her. "You told me you love me, Atif, why?"*

*"Kapri..." I began walking toward her. It seemed as if the more I walked, the further apart we became. "Please..."*

*"I told you, Atif." Michaela's hand rubbed across my chest soothingly. "Kapri can't do the things to you that I can. She won't, baby. We should be together. Forever," she purred, running her tongue across my earlobe.*

*"STOP!" I pushed her away from me. "Kayla, what the fuck wrong with you?"*

*"Atif, you promised!" Free's nagging voice called to me from near the ocean's edge. I spun around to see her reaching for me with her face still bloodied and missing three front teeth. "YOU PROMISED!"*

*"No, Atif, I love you!" Michaela screamed, shifting my face back so I was looking her in the eye. From my peripheral I saw a rope dangling lackadaisically around her neck...*

"Kapri? Kapri, where are you?" I searched for her as the sunbeams faded behind the ocean and the moon's rays bathed the sand in a harsh glow. Squinting, I combed the beach trying to catch a glimpse of her or one of the boys so they could plead my case. Looking around, they were nowhere in sight. "KAPRI!"

I tried moving my hands, but I suddenly couldn't. My limbs weren't cooperating with the commands I was sending from my brain; I felt bound, frozen. I couldn't move my head. I couldn't move my neck. Most importantly, I couldn't find her. I needed her. I needed my wife.

A handsome little boy walked up to me and tugged at my shirt as I stood frozen confusedly in place. My eyes darted downward at his full head of thick, curly hair, and for some reason I felt safe. "Excuse me, Mr. Atif. Do you know where my mommy is?"

As many women as I knew, ran through, and threw away, this kid could be talking about anybody. "Naw, little man, I don't."

He dropped his head as I took in his features. A curiosity in his eyes was recognizable in an area of my brain that I allowed to lay dormant. There was a mysteriousness about him overall, yet there was also an intimateness that I felt deep down. His big brown eyes flickered with grey flecks, and skin the color of the strong Turkish coffee that reminded me of my childhood. I knew this kid from somewhere...

"Everything's gonna be okay, Mr. Atif." His face turned upward a second time and smiled brightly at me, briefly reaching out to wrap his little hand around my pinky finger before he continued on his quest.

"Aye, good luck finding your ol' G, shorty," I called out as he skipped further down the beach.

"Oh, I know where she is," he smiled mischievously. "Stay strong..." His last word was lost on the strong winds suddenly blowing off the water.

Looking around, I noticed Free and Michaela disappeared into thin air...

Prince texted me earlier, letting me know that he was getting together the paperwork to have my baby moved from Milwaukee to the suburbs in the city, but he couldn't tell me where just yet. I had to make sure he was safe before I left, so I tucked in the uncomfortable chair next to his bed as best as I could before drifting off into a fitful sleep. There was so much I wanted to say to him, so much that he needed to know. I had questions that only he could answer, such as what was the real story with him and Free. Why was he in Milwaukee in the first place? What happened that landed him in the hospital?

*"Kapri," Atif's voice called out to me from what looked like a beach setting at night. The moon was high in the sky as he stood in the sand completely still.*

*"Atif?"*

*"Kapri...baby, I love you so much." He snapped out of his daze and headed in my direction. "Please don't leave me."*

*"Atif, you have to pull through. I need you. Me and the boys need you. Our child..."*

*"Our child?"*

"*I'm pregnant,*" *I whispered as his hand reached out to palm my flat stomach.* "*We're gonna have a little girl issuing out orders to her daddy in eight months.*"

*Atif's facial expression was priceless as his head tilted slightly to his right side, staring over my shoulder. Turning to follow his gaze, I noticed a small spot further down the beach as it bobbed up and down on the sand.* "*It's a boy,*" *he spoke longingly; his hand reaching up in slow motion to cover his mouth.*

"*How do you know?*"

"*I know. Kapri...*"

*Reaching up to touch his face, I rested my hand on his cheek as he closed his eyes and leaned in to my touch before his figure began to fade.* "*Atif, don't leave me. Please,*" *I whispered hoarsely as his figure became harder for me to see against the night's sky.* "*Atif...stay with me. Stay with me, baby...Please don't leave me...*"

"*Kapri, I love you,*" *his voice came back to me from the other side as he faded from sight...*

"AAAAAHHHHH!" I felt myself screaming as I bolted upright from my very realistic dream. *It had to be a dream, right?* Looking wildly around the room as the nurse burst through the doors, my vision landed on my husband and my heart broke when I noticed the wetness streaking down the corners of his closed lids.

"Mrs. Hermes, are you okay?" she questioned timidly, gingerly tiptoeing to where my heart was beating out of my chest.

"Yes...yes, I'm fine," I breathed quickly, watching Atif like a hawk. "Can you...can you check his vitals? I need..."

"To put your mind at ease. I know, honey," she spoke quickly, whipping the stethoscope from around her neck, swiftly pressing it against his chest as she watched the screens monitoring his heartrate and respirations. "Everything looks okay as far as I can tell."

"Are you sure?"

The nurse pulled the small chair next to the door near where I sat, slowly slipping into a rabbit hole in my mind created solely from the worrying feeling deep in the pit of my stomach. "I don't know you personally, but I know what you're going through, sweetheart." She took a deep breath in, holding it before allowing the air to escape her chest. "My husband was battling cancer for a long time before his body succumbed to the disease. I've sat in many a hospital rooms just watching, alone with my thoughts. I know..." her voice trailed off.

"How...how did you handle it?" I sniffed, wiping my nose with a Kleenex from the box next to his bed.

"Barely. You see on TV these people surrounding the hospital bed, the gentle doctor coming in to console you and tell you how it's gonna be okay. Next scene these folks going home. It don't happen like that. Reality is, you go through a lot of long nights, a lot of prayer. Your mind plays tricks on you. If your mate is truly your soulmate, you see him in your dreams. That's what..." She paused, watching Atif's chest rise and fall with the melodic beeping of the machines. "...that's what keeps you sane; that's where you want to be, where you want to stay. If he loves you, you feel that love transcending reality. If he loves you, he'll tell you that you can't stay."

"Why? Why can't I stay? Stay with him, stay with my love— the only man who has been created for me? WHY CAN'T I STAY, ATIF!"

"You have to go on, suga," she practically whispered. "You have family who needs you, friends that need you. A baby that needs you. If it's meant to be, he'll be back. Know that this man loves you more than life though," she soothed.

"How do you know?"

The nurse stood up and brushed off her uniform, smiling gently in Atif's direction, adjusting the sensor on his arm that fed his body's natural responses to the monitors surrounding his hospital bed. "These screens tell a story. From looking over his chart and watching as he gets stronger and stronger by the hour, I can tell you for a fact that this man was at death's door when he was admitted. Any person, man or woman that has that much fight in them is fighting for a reason." She turned her gaze back to me. "Give me a call if you need anything, hun," she spoke before disappearing through the door as quietly as she came in while I pinched myself to make sure this was real.

Standing to my feet, I tiptoed to where my husband laid still, resting my hand on his chest first before traveling slowly up his body to touch his cheek as I did in my dream. Knowing he was fighting for me, fighting for us, put my mind at ease for a small corner in time. "Come back to me, Atif." Leaning down, I caressed his lower lip with the tip of my tongue before pressing my lips against his, and I could've sworn he returned my gesture. "I love you. Come back to me, baby." Waiting for his eyes to flutter open, my heart sank a half inch lower in my chest when he didn't. I took comfort in knowing that although he was still in critical condition, he was still alive and still fighting for us.

# SEVEN

# TANJI

I was LIVID. I didn't say anything to Prince, mainly because I was sure he could feel my anger built up inside of me, ready to explode. When we went to get the kids, me and Steve's mother had words, and they weren't "Are you okay?" either. Then the white woman had the audacity to be sitting next to her with that condescending ass smirk, looking down her nose at me as if she was better than me. This bitch didn't know my background. All she knew was what my late husband told her. Yeah, my family might be a little bougie, but so what? I didn't work on the west side of the city for nothing; she could very easily catch this fade too.

After we got back to the condo, I saw that I had a few missed calls from Steve's commanding officer. Sucking up my bad mood, I hit the voicemail to see what he wanted. Maybe it was something small that I could address quickly.

3:33 p.m.: *Good afternoon, Mrs. Houston. This is Admiral Wiggins, and I was just giving you a call to give you an update. We have determined that the child belonging to Tangelica Morse is not the child of Master Chief Petty Officer Houston. Furthermore, we have been unable to find any paperwork to substantiate Ms. Morse's claim that the property owned by Master Chief Petty Officer Houston located in Norfolk is in fact her domicile. Therefore, you are free to....*

3:35 p.m.: *My apologies ma'am, the phone cut off. Just wanted to let you know that the United States Navy is fully prepared to pay out the monies on the insurance policy. Seeing as how Master Chief Petty Officer Houston has listed you as a co-owner on the property, upon his death his entire estate reverts to you as his spouse. We'll just need you to fill out the paperwork. As we all know, that's just a formality. Give me a call here at the base if you have any questions. Enjoy your day, ma'am.*

"Twerk. Twerk. Twerk. Twerk." I stood on the nearest piece of furniture and dropped it low, making my booty bounce on Prince's coffee table as I listened to the message. The kids were asleep anyway. They didn't need to see me releasing my ratchet side and letting it fly all over this condo. "YAAASSS, TANGELICA MORSE! Thirsty BITCH! That wedding ring ALWAYS gonna reign supreme!" I grabbed a bottle of champagne from the refrigerator and popped the cork, letting it spill into the sink a little before taking it to the head.

"Tanji, what you got going on in here?" I heard Prince's keys jingle in the lock before I got a chance to clean myself up. "You drinking without me? Who you got in here?"

"Hey...nobody, love." I wiped my mouth with the back of my hand before cracking a smile in his direction. "Guess what though?"

"What?"

FINALLY I could share a piece of my life with my man without the God beating me to it. "I got a call from the Navy and they said..."

"Tangelica ain't got no kids by your husband," he finished, tossing his keys on the coffee table. "Why is there footprints and a crack in my glass?"

"DAMN, PRINCE!" I was frustrated. Every bit of good news I had, he heard first. He could at least pretend like he didn't know. "Who else know?"

"Tanjalyn, you keep forgetting that we got connections everywhere," he spoke quietly. "I don't wanna know half the shit I know, but if I don't it could be the difference between life and death. You see my brother laid up in a hospital in Milwaukee, fighting for his life, don't you? That's because he knew TOO much, he got too comfortable. He didn't realize his enemy was right there..."

"Prince? What happened to Atif?"

He shook his head and walked away, throwing up his hands as if he'd said too much. "Not for me to say, Tanji. Some shit goes on that you won't know about. I'm out here in these streets and I can't tell you everything that goes on out there. I have to be able to separate this..." he turned and pointed back and forth between us, "...from that." He pointed outside before disappearing to our bedroom.

"Isn't that the main reason Kapri is sitting in a hospital in Milwaukee, crying her eyes out?" I yelled at his back. "Prince, I don't want that to be my life! I don't want to get that phone call saying that you might not make it and I need to get my ass to a hospital!"

"What you saying, Tanji?" Prince came from the back with a towel wrapped around his waist. "I'm not forcing you to stay. You know where the door is."

I was mad as hell, but I ain't gonna lie like Prince couldn't get me pregnant a second time as he stood in the entryway to the living room, glaring harshly in my direction with his toothbrush halfway in his mouth. My eyes instinctively roamed down to his print, which was semi hard and beginning to poke through the towel. "I'm not saying that. All I'm saying is..."

"Nah, you should probably go." He moved closer to where I stood, stopping briefly to put his toothbrush on the island in the kitchen separating us. "If you not sure that you can live this life, I don't wanna come home one day and you gone with my baby. I'd have to hunt you down and kill your ass if that happened," he spoke, running his fingers through my hair.

"Prince..."

"Hmm..." he growled, pressing his manhood against me as he

moved my hair before leaning down and placing soft kisses along the back of my neck.

"I'm not..." I felt my shirt lift up from the back before his lips mashed against my spine. His hands reached around and palmed my breasts as his tongue traced circles on my back. "Prince I'm..."

"See you later, Tanji. I'll drop the kids off tomorrow." He stood up and smacked me on my booty cheek before grabbing his toothbrush and heading back in the bathroom. I heard the faucets turn on and the shower came to life in the glass stall.

Storming to the bedroom where he was humming in the shower, I tried turning the knob to find it locked. "Open this damn door, Prince! What you mean you dropping the kids off tomorrow? Where I'm going? Prince? PRINCE!" I was going to beat on the door until he opened it. Can you believe this man left me standing there for ten minutes while he got clean?

"You calmed down yet?" he questioned nonchalantly when he finally decided to let me in.

"Why can't you be normal, like most men? Why we gotta go back and forth, playing these games?" I yelled. I wasn't used to THIS Prince. The Prince I was accustomed to I saw for a few hours, then we went our separate ways. Who was this man I birthed a child with?

"'Cause I ain't no normal type of muthafucka, that's why. Yo' ass wasn't chasing me down, popping out from behind bushes, pulling up on me in rental cars, fucking me behind yo' friend's back because I was an average nigga. If that's what you want, like I said before, there go the door. Go get hubby's military money and cop you a house out in the 'burbs. Just don't think my baby going with you."

"Why you talking to me like this?" I cowered at his words. Prince wasn't yelling, but from the tone of his voice, I wished he was. For some reason I preferred to be in a position where we were going insult for insult. It was obvious that wasn't who I was dealing with.

"I'm confused on why none of y'all can understand..."

"Y'all? Who the fuck is 'y'all'?"

"...that when a man comes home from being in the streets, you supposed to be his peace! Not questioning, not judging, not nagging! You supposed to be his fucking PEACE! I came in here ready to take a shower, get my dick sucked probably, hit something, and go to bed! Instead, I come in here to a crack in my fucking table that I had flown in from Marrakech, you hyped up off some money you getting from ANOTHA NIGGA, and questioning me about my brother who is in a life or death situation! Instead of you asking me if there was any news on his condition, is he gonna be okay, yo' ass wanna gossip about what the fuck happened! TANJI, I SAW THIS MAN GET HIS SKULL CAVED IN! YOU THINK I WANNA TALK ABOUT THAT SHIT!"

"Uhmm..."

"HUH? ANSWER ME!"

"I...I don't..."

"EXACTLY! NOW TAKE YO' ASS ON! I'LL DROP THE KIDS OFF IN THE MORNING!" he roared before pushing me out the bedroom and slamming the door in my face.

*Be careful what you wish for next time, Tanjalyn,* I cursed myself out as I looked around for my phone. *Prince is NOT Steve.* Now where I'm supposed to go?

# EIGHT

## PRINCE

I had Atif moved from Milwaukee to a house in Hoffman Estates about two weeks ago, and he was getting better. The private doctor that we hired said the swelling had gone down, and it was up to Atif on when he would come out of the coma. Once that happened, he still might have to go through therapy to learn how to do the basic things that we all took for granted, like walking, talking, and the simple stuff to get through the day to day. Atif's father had the best speech pathologist in the world on standby for when that time came, as well as a gang of medical experts to be sure his son got the best care. I wouldn't have expected anything less.

We had the house surrounded for a half a mile with shooters. Anyone that looked suspicious, the snipers had orders to move on sight. Kapri barely left his side unless she was being seen for her prenatal visit. Papa Hermes wasn't taking no chances when it came to his first grandchild; he had an OB/GYN on the property PLUS paid for Kapri's brothers' therapist to come out once a week so they didn't miss any sessions. I filled him in on their situation, and he surprised me when he said he and Atif spoke about it before the incident. He was the one Atif talked to when he was

debating on how to handle Kapri's mother. Not debating a conversation, you gotta remember we talking about father and son street
kings. They were debating on whether or not he should slit her
throat first THEN kick her off the pier or tie her to the anchor.
Atif went with Papa Hermes' idea; it was 'more humane' in his
opinion.

Fucking Tanji. I ain't talked to her since the night I put her out
my house. Matter of fact, this the first time it had been a minute since
we spoke. Yeah, I told her I was gonna drop the kids off, then I
changed my mind. I even kept Steve Jr. She needed to go somewhere
and get her mind right quick, because I wasn't gonna play the same
games with her that her husband did. Tanji needed to understand
above all that I wasn't that nigga; I moved WAY differently. And if
she couldn't get that through her head, I was sure there was somebody out here that could.

Stepping inside the house, I gave Kapri a hug and dapped up her
little brother, Jacari. This lil' dude had a lot of heart. If it wasn't for
Atif, I'm sure the streets would've whispered in his ear by now. Her
younger brother still played with Legos, but it was something about
the way Jacari moved, even as a little kid, that said he should be on
the block. Sometimes you ran into those types of kids; the ones that
the street already had a grip on before they could bust their first nut.
Maybe now with some stability in his life, his future would be
different.

"Hey, Prince. You and Tanji ain't made up yet?" Kapri greeted
me first before heading back inside the mini mansion in the middle of
nowhere.

"Not yet. You know how she can get. That's my bitch and she
stuck with me. How's my brother doing?"

"Better," she said, but the look on her face said something else.
"The doctor says it could be any day now."

"They been saying that since he got here. All them machines he
hooked up to and they ain't got no better news?"

"No. Prince, the doctor asked me if..."

"MRS. HERMES! MRS. HERMES, COME QUICK!" the nurse yelled from Atif's room.

Kapri stopped in mid-sentence, darting towards Atif's room where the woman was gripping the crucifix around her neck and praying in Spanish. Papa Hermes burst into the room right behind us where Kapri was standing in the middle of the space in tears.

"Hey, baby," she managed to get out, creeping to where Atif was watching her with his eyes wide open. "How you feeling?"

"Get that tube out of his throat!" Papa Hermes commanded. "The heir to the throne is back!"

Leaping into action, the doctors gingerly removed the tube from his throat, and the nurse fed him ice chips to soothe any pain he might be in. Staring at the stitches that ran along the top of his head, I was reminded of that day in Milwaukee when Eisha swung a pillow-case with three bricks from the backyard and busted him in the back of his head. Blinking the scene out of my mind, I smiled as I stood with his family, waiting on him to say something.

"Ka..." he stopped to try and clear the hoarseness from his throat, "Ka...Kapri. I love you."

"I know, baby. I know." she wept tears of joy by his side. Wrapping her hand in his, she rubbed the back of his hand against her face with her eyes closed.

Papa Hermes spoke to the doctor in a foreign language; I wish I would've paid my own father some attention when he tried to teach me Armenian and Greek. Even Atif could carry on a conversation with the moneymakers with ease. "Son. Are you up to having a chat with your old man?"

Atif nodded his reply, and they cleared the room. They even put me out.

"So, what do you think Papa is saying to my husband?" Kapri wondered as we stepped into the foyer together.

"Not sure. Atif an' 'nem from the old country, so it ain't no telling," I spoke.

"Maybe he's telling him that I got too much going on and he

shouldn't be with me," she shuddered. Kapri loved the hell out of her some Atif, and judging from his first words when he woke up from a near death coma, the feeling was mutual.

"Don't get your baby's grandfather killed." I chuckled. "Big Guap ain't trying to hear that shit."

"Atif might not want to hear it..."

We both stopped when the butler came to let me know I was being summoned back to Atif's room. "I'll catch up with you before I leave, sis." I jogged to the room where Atif was sitting up and actually looking semi-healthy. "Whaddup, G? How you feeling?"

"Like I been ran over by a Mack truck and they just now put my body back together on some Mr. Potato Head bullshit," he chuckled, rubbing his neck. "Aye, on some real shit, where's Free?"

"Tied up in a basement on 76<sup>th</sup> and Marshfield, waiting on you to wake up."

"Let her go," Papa Hermes spoke rigidly. "She has no business being tied up in a cold, damp basement considering who she is."

Something told me Free's anger had something to do with Eisha and God's conversation in that house that day, but I wanted to hear it from one of them. "Why? Who is she?"

"She's my fucking wife," Atif spoke quietly with his head down.

Papa Hermes nodded in agreement as my brother turned to stare angrily out the bay window to his right with his jawline tight.

"Your wife, Atif?" Kapri pushed the door opened and stormed inside. "When were you gonna tell me you're fucking married?"

Shit was about to get real interesting in Hoffman Estates.

# NINE
## ATIF

I should've just stayed my ass in that coma. At least then I didn't have to explain to my soon to be wife that I was still married and about to commit bigamy because that's how much I loved her. Damn, I should've never walked in that house. That whole thing was a set up. Eisha muthafuckin' ass...wait 'til I get my hands around her throat.

"Well, well, well, if it isn't the God himself." Eisha clapped as I walked through the back door.

Prince wasn't answering his phone and he was right across the street. Probably on the phone lovemaking with his girl. I checked for my heater before I walked in the house, and if I had to use it on her, then fuck it.

"Where's Free?"

"Where's Prince?"

"Bitch, you can't answer a question with a question," I yelled. "Where the fuck is Thotisha?"

"Oh, now she Thotisha, but when you was licking that box like an emotionally broken man on bath salts she was that deal, huh?" this bitch chuckled.

"Licking that box? Bitch, please, the God ain't never licked that bitch's box! The fact that your auntie would tell you some shit about me and her should give you an idea on who the emotionally broken one was!" I smirked. "Since you all in the room, holding the light while we fucked, ask Thotielle about who used to like being R. Kelly'ed: me or her."

"Why would you say something like that about my aunt? She is a saint!"

"Yeah, in Satan's church. Where is she, by the way?"

"She the one who started calling you God, didn't she?" Eisha ignored my question to be nosy. "Had yo' ass gone in the head, didn't she?"

"Nah, you looking at the man who created me. I AM the God of the Chi, baby. Anybody try and claim my fame fucked up in the head. Speaking of which, you ain't told me where Free at yet."

"Ain't you God? Use your all-seeing eye to figure it the fuck out!" she snickered.

"You know what, lil' bitch?" I grabbed her around her neck and slammed her against the nearest wall before I growled in her ear. "You an' that bitch Free gonna stop fucking playing with me. First, you call yourself setting me up with these dirty ass 'angels', now you up in here defending a hoe that don't give a fuck about nobody, including you. Now if you don't want me to punch yo' ass in yo' muthafuckin' mouth, you'll tell me if the bitch is at her house in Menomonee Falls or if she somewhere else. You 'bout to stop playing with me before I kill yo' ass and leave your dead body in this fuckin' house to rot, you hear me!"

"She...she in Menomonee Falls wit' my mama and my other auntie," she choked on her tongue as her eyes bulged slightly out of the sockets.

"That was easy, wasn't it?" I let her go, but not before muffing her head, laughing when she fell to the floor. "I'm just trying to figure out why WE having this conversation in the first place."

"What you mean?" Eisha coughed from her spot on the floor.

"You and Free trying to overthrow the God. This what it is, though?"

"You know what you did, God! Free didn't like that shit one bit!" Her crooked finger shook crazily at me.

"You talking about back home? Free was the dirty one, not me! Wait, why the fuck am I explaining myself to you?"

"Because I'm the one you need to be talking to! I'll take the info back to my auntie..."

I snickered as she sat her goofy ass on the floor, talking 'bout how somebody needed to go through her to talk to my own shabby ass wife. "Girl, fuck you." I waved her off, walking to the door.

"Why...why did you do it, Atif?"

"Do what? Me and your aunt's marriage was arranged back in the old country; I ain't never fucked with her like that!"

"Not..." She coughed for a few seconds before finishing what she was trying to say. "Not that. Why did you kill Hamm?"

"Hamm? You asking me about Hamm?" I cackled in her face. "Fuck you wanna know about that nigga?"

"Hamm was..." she coughed a few more times before catching her breath, "...Hamm was my father."

"Your father? Nah, yo' daddy was some nigga that got locked up in Statesville they called Dino. He was from somewhere in K-Town; they got him when he beat a murder case after serving a year with his snitch ass. Hamm ain't yo' daddy."

"My mother used to fuck around with Dino from time to time, but Hamm was my biological father," she smirked, stumbling to get up from the floor. It wasn't a secret that Hamm didn't mind his customers fucking for payment, but her revelation had me thinking: not only was Eisha and Kapri's little brother half brother and sister, but this nigga was out here just hitting everybody raw and not giving a fuck. He could've had something he couldn't get rid of. How long had this man been a predator?

"So? From where I stand, I did yo' ass a favor. You should be on your knees thanking me if anything. Tell yo' smut ass aunt to give this *beef shit up before she get killed. I ain't forgot the reason why I don't want none of that maggot infested pussy of hers no more,"* I grumbled as I headed for the door.

*"So you ain't got shit to say for why you killed my father?"* Eisha yelled suddenly. *"Why you would take him out of my life? Why he deserved to die?"*

*"BECAUSE I'M GOD, THAT'S WHY!"* I yelled. *I ain't have to explain myself to this young thot; after all I did for her and this was what I got back? Fuck this bitch. "Back the fuck up for a boss before I make good on that threat!"*

*Eisha stepped out of the way for me to walk out the front door. Heading to the truck, I heard footsteps come up behind me and a whooshing sound before something hard collided with my skull. "God, huh. See you in hell, bitch."*

"ANSWER ME, ATIF!" Kapri was screaming off to my left side. I knew I fucked up, but I had to face this woman and give her an explanation at the least.

"I was gonna tell you on the plane," I began. "I was gonna have the ceremony and give you a promise..."

"A promise ring, Atif? A PROMISE RING!" she screamed, kicking the monitor that alerted the medical staff of my heart rate. "Who the fuck you think I am, Snow White? Fucking Cinderella? DO I LOOK LIKE ONE OF THEM FAKE ASS DISNEY PRINCESSES TO YOU, ATIF!"

"A promise that I'd take care of this situation in the next few weeks," I tried to explain, even though Kapri wasn't trying to hear anything I said. I had to at least try before she left me. "Kapri, that's the only thing I've ever kept from you."

"You love me, right?" She chuckled bitterly, nodding while the daggers from her stares should've put me in a coffin. "You love me though, right, Atif? Let me get out this house before I go off on you! Oh yeah, by the way, WE PREGNANT!"

"I know."

"How you know, Atif? HOW YOU KNOW!" She flew in my face screaming.

"You told me. We was on the beach and you told me. I told you it was a boy." My voice broke in front of my father, my right hand mans, the doctors...none of them mattered if she wasn't gonna be in my life.

"I hate you! I HATE YOU, ATIF!" She broke down, sitting in my lap as she sobbed. Wrapping my arms around her, I allowed her to get her anger out. The anger that I caused. Kapri screamed in my hospital gown with me gripping her as best as I could, considering I just came out of a coma. "Atif, I hate you. I hate you. I hate you..."

"I know, baby." I rubbed her hair and kissed her forehead. "I know."

The doctor came over and helped her off my lap as the nurses hooked me back up to the heart monitor. "I'm...I'm not sure whether to call you Mrs. Hermes, or..."

"She's Mrs. Hermes. Respect my muthafuckin' wife fo' we get yo' ass up outta here, homie," I growled, my blood pressure rising.

"Okay, Mrs. Hermes, we need to tend to our patient," the nurse spoke soothingly. "Can you all give us some time to do what you guys pay us to do?"

Kapri bolted out the room first, followed by Pop and Prince who took his time leaving. "Atif."

"Yeah."

"Michaela and Eisha both dead."

"Aight." I nodded, resuming my stare over the green field right outside the bay window as he left. Eisha...good riddance. Michaela though...Prince was gonna have to get me more information on that one. Looking around for my phone, I made sure it was powered on and waited for his text. Judging from his tone, I'd have that information later on today; I wasn't worried about that. What I was worried about was the look on Kapri's face when she told me she hated me. I needed her now more than ever, especially since the whole time she sat in my lap, I hadn't felt a thing.

# TEN

# KAPRI

Who do I call? Who do I lean on? Who can I trust? My best friend belongs to someone else. I was tired of being in relationships where I was the only one trying to work it out. A promise? Atif was gonna fly me all the way to Miami for a promise? He was gonna buy me a beautiful house on Fisher Island overlooking the ocean, give me a big, beautiful princess cut diamond for a promise?

I was tired of giving chances and giving my heart away only to be given back excuses. I needed to let Atif go so he could go do this dumb shit to somebody else. Somebody more deserving than me, like some of the bucket headed bitches he used to fuck around with before me. Monica, Tanji's sister-in-law, was one of those women; maybe she still had a shot. Me and Atif could co-parent.

Sitting in the room in the middle of the king-sized bed, I cried until the tears dried up on my cheeks. This wasn't what I thought my life with Atif would be. He wasn't supposed to be married. He was supposed to be mine. He was supposed to be the man I wished for every night my mother came in the house high out of her mind, demanding that I do things and allow strange men to do things to me that I couldn't stop. He was supposed to be the man who accepted me for all of my flaws, and loved me despite my past. He was supposed to be the man who had no problem sitting down and talking through our problems, not hiding his past while I put my life on display open for him to inspect. Atif was supposed to love me. ATIF WAS SUPPOSED TO LOVE ME!

Pulling out my phone, I downloaded the Uber app and requested a ride. Since we were so far out, the closest driver was forty-five minutes away. I was fine with that, because it gave me time to get my stuff together. I didn't know where I was going, but I did know wherever it was wasn't here. Grabbing my suitcase from underneath the bed, I started emptying the dresser drawers before a knock at the door had me wiping my eyes. Heading to answer the knock first, I cracked the door opened then headed to the closet to finish grabbing my things.

"How are you holding up...wait, are you leaving?" Papa Hermes questioned with his eyebrow raised.

"No offense Mr. Hermes..."

"Call me Papa. My son is in love with you."

"You know, I find it funny how you had me in here feeling like I was a part of the family, calling me your daughter, making sure my little brothers were taken care of, got us out here in this damn house and everything, KNOWING your son was already married! I just hope my baby doesn't inherit that familial trait from y'all," I grumbled, pacing between the closet and my bed as I packed my stuff.

"And what trait is that, my dear?" he questioned gently.

"Hypocrisy. You're an even bigger hypocrite than your son!"

"Kapri, normally when anyone speaks to me in this manner, I cut their tongue out for the disrespect," he began calmly, taking a seat in the chair near the door. Crossing his right leg over the left, he leaned back and lit a Cuban cigar, blowing the smoke towards the door before he spoke again. "Since you're pregnant with my legacy, and I know my son's temperament, I'll allow it for now."

"Why are you here, Mr. Hermes?" I stopped, taking a seat on the bed to hear him out.

"I know you don't want to hear anything from my son right now, so I'll tell you why he's married and didn't tell you. Atif and Siranush were promised to one another the day Siranush's father saved my life in the old country. As a matter of fact he's still sitting in a Turkish prison because of me. I never planned to move to the United States, but I was here taking care of some business in New Orleans when I met Atif's beautiful, beautiful mother." He paused for a second, I assume to reminisce on his relationship with my child's grandmother. "Mmm...have you met Philomené?"

"Umm...not yet." I giggled for the first time since I got the news. "She's on a river cruise from Amsterdam to Bucharest. They weren't able to reach her when Atif had his accident. I don't think she knows he almost..."

"It's okay, Kapri. It's okay..." he soothed, reaching over to rub my back.

I collected myself enough to finish our conversation. "I'm looking forward to meeting her one day. Atif speaks so highly of her."

"When you meet her, you'll see what I mean. Mmm...tell my baby I said I miss her too." His eyes glazed over. I hoped he remembered he was in the middle of telling me about Atif and Siranush, AKA Free.

"Papa?"

That snapped him out of his mental trip down memory lane. "Yeah, yeah, so me and Philomené fell into some crazy shit back in the day. She's a southern girl, so I had to propose to her and buy her a house before she'd let me corrupt her, but when I did...mmphf! When you see her, tell her I wanna see her, too." He leaned back in his chair with his eyes rolled in the back of his head.

"Mr. Hermes, you okay?" I didn't know how I felt about Atif's father lusting after his mother in front of me. From where I sat, this man needed a cold shower at the least.

"Yeah, yeah, I'm okay. Anyway, Philomené gave birth to my only child, and for that I'll forever be in love with that woman. I was called back to the old country to face a few weapons charges. The man currently serving time for my crimes made me promise that my son married his daughter for his allegiance. I agreed, and he lied to the high court. Fast forward to when Atif found out about his nuptials, he wasn't happy." Papa chuckled. "I remember the day Atif showed up in Armenia to visit me and found himself standing in front of a wedding officiant with a woman he didn't know standing happily at his side," he snickered. "Nevertheless he did it for me, so that I wouldn't look like a less than an honorable man in front of my comrades."

"If that's what happened, why didn't Atif tra-la-la off with his wife?"

"After they consummated their marriage, Atif suddenly changed his mind and said no. He wasn't going to be told who he could love and who he should love. That girl Eisha was Siran's niece, and since she was from here originally, she would be her liaison here in the states. The original plan was for Eisha to bond with my son on behalf of Siran's family and helping him to set things up here while Siran prepared to move from her beloved Armenia to the US. Instead, she convinced Siran's family that she would speak to Atif about creating an Armenian mob, except all the members would be women. Had anybody asked me, I could've told them it wouldn't work because I know my son, but Eisha convinced her family that she could get Atif on board. Once we found out about this 'God' and him changing Meghranush and Kayiane's names to Gabriella and Michaela, calling them his angels, Siran suddenly came up with a new plan in order to have the city under her rule: to wage war against my son in order to get his attention. My son..." Papa stopped and snickered, "...my son is his father's child."

"None of this changes the fact that he should've told me this back when we first started seeing one another. Before I got my feelings involved. Before he got me pregnant." I sat on the bed as a fresh round of tears started all over again.

"I don't know why he didn't tell you, but if I had to guess, it was to spare your feelings." Atif's father sat on the bed next to me, rubbing my shoulder. "Like I said before, Atif is just like his father, he loves hard. His mother left me years ago, but I would still, to this day, drop everything for her if that's what she wanted. I'd do what I should've done back when she asked me to choose between her and the streets."

"You chose the life over your woman?"

"I'm ashamed to admit it, but yes. Back then I was making so much money...it didn't make sense at the time for me to give it up to be a family man. I wanted both: my woman and my money. Philomené didn't want Atif to follow in my footsteps. Unfortunately, that's exactly what happened. If I had it all to do over again though..." He stroked his beard thoughtfully with a faraway look in his eye.

I allowed my mind to drift off to touch on the what-if in my own relationship. Could I truthfully co-parent with Atif knowing how my heart beats faster when I was in his presence? Would this be my fate once our son grew up; me wishing I could turn the hands of time back to this moment? I didn't know what Papa Hermes had done in his life after Atif's mother left him, but judging from our conversation his life wasn't as glamourous as it seemed. Having all that money and power was nothing if you didn't have someone by your side to share it with. Somebody that had your back while you watched the front. Some-body who cared for you, that face to come home to that you knew was there because they missed YOU. No matter whether y'all had more money than Jeff Bezos or if you were broker than the homeless people on Lower Wacker Drive, you were happy because y'all had each other.

Atif loves me. I know he loves me. Right now, that love isn't enough for me and him to share space. I wasn't in the right mindset to look at his face knowing he was married to someone else, no matter what the circumstances were. "I'm sorry, Papa. I have to go, I can't stay here. Please let Atif know I love him, but I can't do this. I hope you and him understand. I'll be back for my little brothers tomorrow."

"Kapri, I'm begging you. Please don't leave my son. Not right now, he needs you," Papa spoke gently, resting his hands on my shoulders as my phone dinged with the notification from the Uber app.

"Papa, I gotta go." I stood up, zipping up my suitcase and rolling it in front of me. "I'll be back..."

"If you must," he spoke, taking my suitcase from my hand while following me to the front door. As he loaded my luggage into the trunk, he removed a wad of money from his pocket and pressed it into my hand. "Take this. You have my number. Call me if you need the family."

"I doubt..."

"Don't be stupid, Kapri. I can't stop you from leaving. Bad enough you haven't spoken to my son. However, this would be a devastating blow to this conglomerate if anything happened to you and you're pregnant with our legacy," he stressed. "Call us."

"Yes, sir." Hopping in the Toyota Prius, I thanked the driver for being patient before waving at Atif's father as we pulled out of the circular driveway, headed back to the city that, although it caused me so much pain, I couldn't seem to let it go.

# ELEVEN

## TANJI

I begged the people at my old apartment complex to let me move back in after God kicked my door off the hinges, and they told me no. I ended up in an apartment building in the same neighborhood though, so it wasn't too bad. I still couldn't believe they did me like that because before Kapri moved in, I was a model tenant. They never had problems out of me because I was rarely there. I had a marital home and the house left to me by my grandmother before my baby father burned it down to cover up my husband's murder. Even with him dead, I had a home in Jacksonville, Florida and another in Norfolk, Virginia. For now, I stayed in Chicago to figure out what I wanted to do with my life.

At first, I was a little upset that Prince stole my kids, however looking around my one bedroom, I didn't mind. They loved him to death, and he treated them both like a father should. Nothing like what Steve put them through; sometimes he was fully present as a father and husband, other times he was there in body, but not in mind. Lately my son had begun referring to himself as 'Little Zadrian', and although I tried to stop him, Prince told me to leave him alone. Steven Houston might not have been the best father in the world, still that's who he was to my son: his father. I wasn't comfortable with him abandoning his heritage to be accepted by my boyfriend. Judging from Prince's actions, who's to say that our relationship would last?

With Kapri tied up in Atif's health and well-being, I was back to where I was before we met with no one to talk to. As much as I didn't want to, I picked up the phone and dialed Monica's number. There was too much going on in my head, and if I didn't get it out one way or the other, I felt like I would explode.

"Hey, sis, what's going on?" Monica's chipper voice in my ear started a headache at the base of my skull. I had to shake it off before I hung up.

"Hey, you busy?"

"No. You need me to watch the kids? I gotta come over your house because..."

"No, no, nothing like that."

"Oh," she replied dejected. "What's going on?"

"Can you come over? I need someone to talk..."

"Yes, yes, of course I can!" she squealed. "I got some stuff to tell you anyways," her voice dropped to a whisper.

"About?"

"Tangelica."

"Bih, lemme text you the address! I'll see you in a minute." I hurried up and got off the phone. Grabbing a bottle of wine from the refrigerator, I started a Netflix movie and got comfortable.

The ringing of my bell brought me out of my nap; I must've dozed off. "Who is it?" I pressed the button on the intercom and asked.

"Tanji, it's me," Monica's voice called back to me.

I hit the buzzer and listened as she came through the downstairs door. Even though my apartment was on the second floor, I still heard the door open and slam behind her. Leaving the door to my place opened a crack so she could let herself in, I went back to my spot on the couch.

"Girl, that's a lotta stairs," she stopped and caught her breath as she closed the door. "I know you miss your house!"

"I figured I can get my daily workout just coming and going, so it's cool," I replied, patting the couch next to me. "You want something to drink?"

"You got some water?" she wheezed, walking slowly in the living room and taking a seat on the couch next to me.

"I sure do, and it's hot. You got the teabags?" I snickered, getting straight to the point. Monica mentioning Tangelica's name earlier had my interest piqued ever since.

"GIIIIIIRLLLL, I don't know what to call her; my brother's fiancé, my brother's girlfriend, my brother's baby mama..."

"You can call her who she is: your brother's hoe." I brought her a bottle of water from the refrigerator. "What happened though?"

"She got my mama wrapped around her little finger," she began, taking a long gulp from the bottle. "Told her Steve was about to divorce you, how she had access to all his personal business, how he got her on some bank accounts that you don't know about, how he put some money up for her and her baby..."

"You talking about that baby that ain't his?" I snickered with no shame. I couldn't believe for all his conniving to make sure I didn't get nothing because I cheated on him in our marriage, he was the one out here looking like a fool. Tangelica was fucking my husband way longer than I was fucking Zadrian.

"What you mean, that baby ain't his?"

"Girl, the military don't release death benefits for a dependent unless it's proven that the child is a dependent of one of their own," I shared what Admiral Wiggins left on my voicemail. "Steve ain't signed no birth certificate."

"She got paperwork, though. Something from DNA Diagnostics that say he's 99.97% her daughter's father."

"You know they out here faking DNA tests too, right? Did she submit that to the military?"

Monica stopped in mid drink. "I...I don't...well you'd think she would, right? Considering that it would prove her claim. She should know Steve didn't sign that baby's birth certificate, right?"

"I don't speak hoe-anese, so I wouldn't know." I grabbed the bottle of Moscato and popped the top, pouring myself a glass. "If she got all that proof, she should be good then."

"Speaking of proof, she say she got a video that proves you had Steve killed." Monica poured herself a glass of wine as well. "Said she gonna send it to the police as soon as she get back to her laptop."

"Tell her good luck with that," I spoke firmly, hoping Monica didn't see my hand suddenly begin to shake. Steve told Prince he had cameras in both houses, that's how he knew I was cheating on him. It was possible that he gave his little tramp access to these cameras if they existed.

The fire department contacted me and told me that they were still investigating the fires; I didn't know whether or not they found Prince's phone or if it melted in the rubble. Either way, I couldn't collect the insurance money for the properties until their investigation was complete. I didn't want to be implicated in this mess; I had no way of knowing that Prince and God would stage a break in to kidnap my baby. God knows I never thought Steve would be dead behind that kidnapping. If she did have a video, it would put my man and his brother away for the rest of their lives, and I couldn't allow that to happen either. I had to talk to this Tangelica to find out what, if anything, she knew and handle her accordingly.

"Tanji, you okay?" Monica's voice pulled me out of my thoughts.

"Yeah, girl, I'm fine. All this talk about Steve...I just miss him so much."

She sighed, scooting over to the couch to give me a big hug. "I know you loved my brother, sis," Monica consoled. "You're still grieving, and this woman comes out of nowhere talking about how her and Steve were in love. That has to hurt."

"Nobody understands the struggles of a wife, you know what I mean?" I found a few tears to drop, rocking back and forth as she went to find some tissue. "We go through so much! Then for this woman to come along and accuse me of this...killing my own husband? I mean, it's bad enough she OBVIOUSLY knew about me this whole time, but for her to say these things about me?" I was in full hysterics by the time she got back. "And then for your mother to BELIEVE her? That hurts, Monica!"

She nodded in agreement, trying to comfort me through my alleged pain. "I know, Tanji. Girl, I know. I told my mama she was wrong..."

"I've NEVER done anything for your mother to think I would kill my own husband! Why, Monica? WHY!" I yelled, wiping the tears from my eyes and blowing my nose.

"I think she just wanted some mixed grandkids, to be honest," Monica revealed. "She always talking about how pretty that baby's skin and hair is."

"Jenesis..." I started, then stopped. Prince was half Armenian, just like God, so our baby WAS mixed. Jenesis wasn't her grandchild, though. Not biologically, she was his legal child; Steve signed HER birth certificate. "Monica..."

"Everybody been knew Jenesis was Prince's daughter," she spoke. "We was just waiting to see when you'd say something. The girl look just like him."

"I wasn't trying..."

"Steve been cheating on you for YEARS. Tangelica ain't the first. Ain't nobody surprised that you went out and got you somebody on the side too," she counseled.

A weight lifted off my shoulders, however Prince's words to me about Steve's mama trying to bait me still rang in my ears. "I loved your brother though, Monica. No matter what we went through, I loved my husband."

"I know, sis."

Pouring myself another glass, I remembered that I needed to switch to water before I ended up folded on this couch and telling this girl about how I knew who killed her brother for real. "So what else is going on in y'all family?" I hurried and changed the conversation.

"Well, you know my mama..." she began, and I tuned her out. I really didn't care about her Uncle Mack who preferred to be called Auntie Michelle, nor did I want to know about how her cousin Yemi was pregnant with twins by the same nigga who beat her ass every other day. I was two seconds from putting her out before she said something that made my ears perk up.

"...pregnant by God. You know him too?"

"What?"

"I said I'm pregnant by God. We used to meet up from time to time, then he just stopped coming around. Last time I saw him, we didn't use nothing and I missed my period. Since him and Prince always together, I was wondering if you knew where I could find him," she spoke quietly.

The glass I was holding slipped out of my hand, crashing against the floor, and jolted me out of my temporary shock. All this shit sitting on this table, and her ass was still thirsty. "Uhhh...no, I don't. I'll ask Prince next time I see him though."

"Let me know, okay?"

"Mmhmm," I called behind me, heading to the kitchen for the broom and mop. Like I said before, every time Kapri got her a corner of happiness, it turned to shit. I had to call Prince.

# TWELVE
## PRINCE

"That shit didn't even sound right when you said it: Michaela killed herself." Atif was on FaceTime, stroking his beard. I'd just gave him the information Jeff gave me that day I met him out south. "She might've been upset, but I knew when you texted me that bullshit about her hanging herself, that shit was staged."

"I'm just trying to figure out why though. Why would they do that to her?"

"I know Eisha was a little pissed about you tossing Gabrielle in the garbage," God snickered. "My opinion: she got what she deserved, with her snitch ass."

"What that have to do with Kayla though?"

"You know how these bitches set up. Call Monte and see if he can shed some light on the situation with Gabrielle and Free's right hand though."

"I'm on it."

"Any word on the misses?"

"Yeah, she got an apartment on the north side, like we ain't got people up there too," I reported. "Kapri stay off of Touhy and Damen in a courtyard building up there."

"Yeah, I know a few gangsters up that way too. Call Quavo and let him know she up there so he can keep an eye on her."

"Will do, God."

"How she find a crib that quick though?" he pondered. When it came to Kapri, Atif needed every detail, even the small ones.

"She found one of them 'ya dig' landlords." I chuckled. "Ones that don't do no credit or background checks if you got enough money, ya dig?"

"Yeah, keep an eye on my wife. Anything happen to her, somebody 'bout to be digging. Anything else?"

"That should be it."

"Hit my line if anything else comes up, especially with the wife. Lemme go deal with these therapy people," he hurried off the phone.

Wiping my hand down my face, I was tired. Tired of dealing with these crazy ass people and this never ending situation with Free and Eisha. Quiet as it was kept though, I was more tired of Tanji playing these fucking games. Her ass was still gone too, and I needed some pussy. Grabbing my phone, I checked to see if the nanny needed anything before I headed out to the west side. I was putting an end to this shit TODAY.

Pulling up across the street from her apartment building in one of my trap cars, I watched for a while to see if anybody looked like they were going to her crib. What she didn't know was that I sat here everyday for an hour or better watching. I loved her hardheaded ass regardless of what she thought. Yeah, I was still pissed about that money she was getting from her husband, however I was sure I could convince her to put that into a trust for Steve Jr. Jenesis was gonna be straight regardless.

I watched as Monica, one of God's ex-slides, came out the building with a smug look on her face. Before I got a chance to wonder what that was about, my phone rang.

"Hey, baby mama. What's good?"

"You know a female named Monica that God used to fuck with?" she asked, getting straight to the point.

"Yeah, why?"

"This sour apple, bitter bitch claim she pregnant by him."

*That was quick,* I thought. "How you know?"

"She just sat on my couch and told me! Why you so calm?"

"Can I come sit on yo' couch and tell you something?"

I could hear the smirk on her face all in her voice. "Depends on what you trying to come over and say."

Rolling up my windows, I got out the car and chirped the alarm twice before jogging across the street. "Buzz me in the building, I can't say it over the phone." I hung up as the buzzer sounded on the downstairs door. Taking the steps two at a time, I pushed the door opened as she sat on the couch, ass naked.

"How you know where I stay, Prince?" she questioned, taking a sip from her glass.

"You know Daddy knows your every move. You missed me?"

"Nope," her lips lied as she watched my dick growing in my jogging pants.

I walked over to where she sat and stood in front of her, blocking her view of the TV. "You didn't miss me, Tanji?"

I put my meat right in her eyeball and she grabbed that boy just like she was supposed to, massaging him through my jogging pants. "Who you been giving my dick to?" she questioned, reaching down in my jogging pants and pulling him out.

"Put him in your mouth and find out," was my reply, watching her spit on him and swallow him whole. Closing my eyes, I rested my hand on the top of her head as she took care of a boss; her slurping had me ready to release my babies down her throat. "FUCK girl! Fuck you been doin'...SHIT!" I shot an army down her esophagus as she pulled her head away from my shit with the thin string of my nut on her lips.

Staring me in the eyes, she licked that off her bottom lip as she laid back on the couch and spread her pussy wide open. "Did you miss me, Prince?" She dipped two fingers inside of her glossy, pink gushy, biting her bottom lip.

"I might've." I shoved myself inside of her, sliding her hips off the couch and tilting her upwards so I could control my thrust. Tanji's legs dangled at my side as our skin slapped together. Her moans had me slamming into her shit harder and harder as she came back to back. "Who you been giving my pussy to, dammit?"

"I...FUCK ME, PRINCE! SHIT!"

"Answer me, Tanjalyn Mariah! Who the fuck you been...FUCK, GIRL!" I nutted all in her shit; wasn't nobody catching my seed except her as far as I was concerned. She shocked the hell out of me when she snatched my shit out of her and sucked the rest of it out of me. I didn't know when my baby mama became bonafide, but I liked that shit.

"Mmm...my Prince so sweet." She licked her fingers and swirled her tongue around her lips one more time.

"You love sucking my dick, don't you?" I collapsed on the couch. Tanji wore me out just that quick; I must be getting old. "Whew, shit! Go get Daddy a bottle of water." I smacked her ass when she stood up; baby must've been living that squat life since she been gone because that muthafucka was sitting up perfecto!

"We need to start back working out together," she called from the kitchen as my eyelids got heavier. "PRINCE!"

"Hmm..."

"Boy, I know you ain't sitting up here sleep off no two damn nuts!"

"Naw, bae, I'm just resting my eyes for a few minutes..." I felt myself drifting off.

"Come on baby, come lay in the bed so you can get some rest." She nudged me gently.

Opening my eyes for a few minutes, I felt her trying to pull me off the couch and helped her out as best as I could. It took everything I had in me to drag me from the living room to her bedroom. Laying in the bed, I felt her tuck me in, giving me a kiss on the cheek before whispering how sorry she was. That's all I was asking for in the first place. *Fuck this shit, Tanji bringing her ass home. I'll just have to pay to break this lease.*

# THIRTEEN

## ATIF

**M**an...a month of sitting in this damn bed, only getting up when these people came in here to take me to therapy for a few hours, doing that swimming pool shit to build my strength back up...all this shit was for the birds. If I didn't have to, I wouldn't be doing none of this shit. I put up with these folks because I knew I had to in order to get back to what the God did best; hit these streets. From trap God getting it out the mud to hood God still out here in the trenches, muthafuckas called me all that and more. I was more than Chi Town's favorite bully; I was Chi Town's most respected God. Anybody referred to me as anything else and they might find themselves on the wrong end of my wrath.

Pop called himself creeping in my room quietly. Funny thing was as quiet as this big ass house was, he sounded like a herd of elephants. "What is it now, Pop?"

"I just wanted to tell you..."

I smelled her perfume before she entered the room; my second favorite lady was here in my presence. "Atif? Or are you still calling yourself God?" my mother asked gently.

"Ma." Using my cane, I eased myself off of the bed and crept towards where she stood in the doorway. She met me halfway, throwing her arms around me to give me a big hug. "When did you get here?"

She cleared her throat and turned to look at my father, who looked away. "That's not important. What is important is that I'm here, right?" She smiled and patted my hand.

"What you..."

"Have the doctors and nurses been taking good care of you, son?" she quickly changed the subject, fussing as she straightened the sheets on my bed.

I stared at my father, who was in the middle of picking an imaginary piece of dust from his shirt, making a performance of shaking nothing from between his fingers with his face frowned up.

"Yeah, ma," I drawled, shaking my head at both of them as I limped back to my hospital bed. "Don't come in here with no damn babies, y'all too old for that shit!"

"Your father tells me the only one around here having some babies is you, son," she giggled, helping me back in bed before pulling the covers up. "Where is my real daughter-in-law? Not that slut you married in Armenia." Her eyes shrunk into slits as she glared briefly at my father.

"Philomené, not now, okay, love? Let's not do this here," Pop cautioned, darting his eyes between me and her.

"Atif doesn't...you're right. You're right. Let me enjoy this time with my son." She calmed down, breathing deeply through her irritation. "How are you, son?"

"Doing a lot better than I was, Ma."

"That's good. My baby has good genes...good genes that he got from my side of the family," she smiled, hugging my neck. "Good genes that he'll pass down to...do we know what we're having?"

"It's a boy."

"Good, strong genes that he'll pass down to my grandson," my mother rejoiced. "Atif, when do I get to meet my daughter-in-law? You never did say."

"Ma, right now it's..."

"I'm here, Mrs. Hermes," Kapri called from the doorway. "Glad I'm finally meeting you. Atif talks about you so much I feel like I already know you."

If my parents weren't in the room, I'd have Kapri bent over this bed, trying my best to give her some of this crooked dick from the back so I could watch that ass clap. That love glow looked good on her chocolate aura when she walked in the room wearing a simple black t-shirt dress with some black girl magic quote written across her full titties. If she had a bra on, it wasn't doing her no justice because I could just make out her nipples pointed towards me, telling me how much they missed being sucked. Her legs were well toned, and I could smell the coconut and lemon oil on her skin as she leaned over and gave my mama a hug. My baby boy had my wife looking like she needed to be ate slowly; needed to take my time with that sweet girl. Them lips though...damn, I missed them lips...

"ATIF!" my mother yelled as my man rubbed against her elbow.

"Huh?"

"Do you and my beautiful daughter need a moment?"

"Yeah, they need a moment," Pop hurriedly interjected. "Come on, Philomené, lemme show you the rest of the house. Let's start with the jacuzzi downstairs in the basement," he smiled slyly as my mother stood up and speed walked to where he stood in the doorway.

"Come show me this jacuzzi you want me to see so bad, Aram," she cheesed, hard. I knew Pop was still hitting that. It was good to see them back together, even if it was just for a little while.

"Take your time, Atif," Pop called out as he shut the door behind him. "Get that apology right!"

"Your parents still fucking, ain't they?" Kapri giggled, listening at my mother yell out like she was still twenty-five as they thundered across the hardwood floors like some kids before slamming the basement door shut.

"That's news to me, but I guess so." I chuckled at the look in Pop's eyes when he offered my mother that tour of the house that only included the fully furnished basement complete with a sauna and jacuzzi tub. "What you been up to, chocolate girl?" I turned my attention back to her. Baby remined me of one of those World's Finest Chocolate bars that I used to buy all the time in the eighth grade; that pussy was just as sweet too.

"Look at you, got redemptions on your mind when you think about me," she giggled, not knowing she was right. I had to do something to get her back.

"Is it working?"

"Maybe." She dipped her head with the saddest look on her face. "Atif..."

"What's wrong, Kapri? Tell me."

"Sitting in that apartment going crazy because..."

"No baby, we can't have you going crazy." I pulled her closer to me, loving when she rested her head on my chest. "Tell the God what you need."

"You." She ran her tongue across my lips. "Can the God bless me with Atif Hermes?"

"Your wish has always been my every command." I stood up without my cane; the pain shooting through my lower body was nothing if I couldn't have her.

"Baby, no. Lay back down, let me take care of you," she uttered, pulling my briefs off slowly. She started to put her mouth on me before I stopped her.

"No."

"No?"

"No."

"Atif..." she looked at me confused.

"You pregnant with my son and you like to swallow."

That was all that needed to be said. Blinking twice, she stood up and pulled her dress over her head. The fact that she was completely naked underneath gave me even easier access to her sexy, pregnant self. "What can we do then?" she questioned sultrily, leaning against me while wrapping her arms around my neck.

Face to face with my favorite meal, I licked my lips as I placed her leg on my shoulder, diving in tongue first. I slipped both hands between her thighs and pressed her ass cheeks closer to my face to hold her in place as I feasted on her sweet pussy. Feeling her hands wrap around my head, she pulled me closer to her as she stood on her toes so I could get a better angle. "Lay down, baby, so your man can suck this pussy the right way."

Sliding in the king-sized hospital bed next to me, she followed my command as I slipped two fingers inside of her sopping wet sex. Maneuvering my digits in and out of her slippery cream had my dick firming up as her pussy went from hot to scalding. "Atif...mmmm... you said....you said you was gonna..."

"What you want me to do, baby?" I leaned in to mumble in her ear as she squirmed with anticipation. "Tell me what you want me to do."

"Atiiiifff," she breathed, knowing how that shit turned me on.

"Tell me you want me to make love to you, Kapri," I moaned, lying down next to her before shifting her body sideways. I wanted her to look me in my eyes as I licked my lips with her on my tongue.

"Baby...is it safe?"

"That's not what I asked you, Kapri," I scolded, lifting her leg to slide inside of her. Resting her thigh on top of mine, I watched her close her eyes, licking her lips as her body shuddered against mine. Reaching around to grab her booty, I pulled her closer to me while squeezing that soft muthafucka. Her little baby bump rubbing against me reminded me to be gentle. "You want me to make love to you, girl? Mmmm...look at all that chocolate though." I leaned in and nibbled on her neck. Damn, she tasted good.

"Atif," she wrapped her hands around my neck, resting her head on my shoulder. "Baby, promise me..."

"Done," I spoke, moving south to nibble on her shoulder. I missed this girl BAD!

"You don't even know..."

"We divorced." I lifted her leg up, trying to do that one move that would have her pussy juices running down my thighs. Her pregnant pussy was already wet as fuck and I hadn't dug in her guts as deep as I wanted to just yet.

She flipped me over on my back and I put my hands up to surrender as she climbed on top. "You divorced?"

"Mmhmm," I moaned, gripping her thighs as she scraped her hips back and forth across my rock hard rod. That box was squishy just like I liked it, and only got wetter the more she glided across my waist.

"Why you ain't text me that?" She licked my chest, cinching her teeth around the tip of my nipple to tickle it with her tongue.

I thrusted my hips upwards as hard as I could, watching as she bounced up and down on my pelvis. "You feel that dick? Feel good in that pussy, don't he? Don't leave me again, Kapri," I growled forcefully.

"Okay...okay...okay, Ati...Atifffff..." She rubbed her clit as she pounced back and forth with her lids closed.

"You want that nut, don't you, baby?"

"Yes," she whimpered, her pussy plopping down on my dick, suctioning him with each stroke.

"Ask me nice and I might give it to you," I ordered. "ASK ME, KAPRI!"

"PLEEEEASE, ATIF?"

"Please what?"

"PLEASE CAN I HAVE...OH, GOOOODDD!" she screamed as her love rained down on me.

I couldn't hold it no more. I bolted upright and held her body close to mine as I shot everything in me up towards her stomach.

"I love you, baby," she whispered over and over, planting peck kisses all over my face.

"You mine, Kapri. Don't you ever forget, you mine, okay?"

"Yes."

"Anybody tell you different, I don't care who it is, I'm putting a bullet in they face, you hear me?"

"Yes."

"Go get cleaned up so we can go for round two." I kissed her on the mouth as she sat up. Throwing her legs across the bed, I watched her head to the bathroom with a smile beaming over her face. I loved making my baby smile, even if it gave me so much pain to do so. My hips and legs were on fire, but it was well worth it. That pussy was good as hell.

## FOURTEEN

## KAPRI

He was the food that fed my soul; I couldn't imagine life without him. Looking back, I can honestly say before him, my relationships were one sided. I'd never been with anyone who was so in sync with both my heart and my mind; that fake love from my past used to seem so real to me. All those times I thought I was hurt, thought I couldn't live without that person's love that the thought of not being with them was what broke me down emotionally. Atif's love to me was pure; I didn't know the man that turned the most hardened criminal into a bitch. No matter what though, he couldn't shake that cockiness, and that only made me love him more.

With him, I wasn't afraid to be vulnerable, and I wanted the same from him. Sitting in that apartment and thinking about Papa Hermes' explanation for Atif's actions, I understood. I originally came to the house to check up on my little brothers, since Atif threatened me from a Bluetooth speaker in the family room when I tried to come and get them before. I knew then that I needed to hear him out. Atif showed me time and time again that he wanted me to be a part of his world; reassuring me with the consistency of his overall presence. Him taking on the responsibility of being the male role model my brothers needed growing up in the Chi solidified it for me. I was all in. He gave me my love confidence. Before him, I never knew what a 'good' man was. I loved Atif Hermes with all my heart and soul, and if it took the rest of my life to prove it, I would.

"You still mad at me?" he murmured in my ear, lying next to me and running his fingers through my hair.

"Yup."

He sat up, staring at me questioningly. "After all that, you still mad? What I do?"

"You in pain but you trying to please me." I put my head down, feeling the tears well up in my eyes. "That's not what I want."

"How you know?"

"Same way you know we having a boy: I know. Now, lay down and let your body heal, will you?" I tucked him in bed, hitting the button to signal his private doctor.

"Stop, Kapri, damn! Yeen gotta call him in here, chill!" he yelled as the nurse entered his suite.

"Yes, Mrs. Hermes?"

"Check him. He insisted that we..."

"KAPRI, CHILL! She ain't gotta know we was in here fucking!"

"I'm sure she already does, the way you was in here moaning and smacking my ass!" I playfully mushed his head, laughing when he turned away trying to pretend like he was embarrassed.

"Mr. Hermes, please listen to your wife," the older woman chuckled. "I'll check your legs, but I'll give you a few minutes before I take your blood pressure," she winked at me.

*Thank you*, I mouthed. Vaguely remembering that my phone rang while me and Atif were playing porn star, I grabbed it from my purse to see who it was. The people who were the most important to me were already at the house, except for Tanji. Opening the text from her, I briefly scanned through, glaring at my fiancé before reading it again. "Atif, baby, where your keys at?"

"To what?"

"I need a car."

"Keys to the Wraith should be in my pocket. Naw, wait, keys to the Wraith at the house. Keys to the Jeep in my pocket. Where you going?"

"I gotta go to the city to grab my stuff from that apartment..."

"Give Prince your keys, he'll get your stuff," he cut me off in mid-sentence.

"...and I'm going to see Tanji for a while."

"Naw...naw..." He shook his head. "I want you here."

"Atif. Really?"

"Free somewhere out there in the world pissed because I had our marriage annulled, Eisha knew about you, and she had her personal assistant pop up on you at the hospital." He ran down his excuses for keeping me near him on one hand. "I won't allow it."

"Baby, Milwaukee is NOT Chicago." I giggled. "That woman wouldn't make it off the expressway, she come looking for me! Have you seen her?"

"Kapri, it don't matter what a muthafucka look like. If they want you dead, yo' ass will be somewhere stankin'. I can't take that kind of a risk with you."

"Then how you let me live in a whole apartment by myself, if that's the case?"

"If I told you how many of your neighbors actually work for me, it'll blow your mind," he chuckled, adjusting himself in the bed. "You were never in any danger in that building, while you over there paying yourself rent."

"What?"

"Girl, I bought the building. You think I was just gonna let you stay there by yourself?"

"ATIF!"

"What?" He looked so innocent sitting in that hospital bed, knowing that was a borderline stalker move.

"If you don't see nothing wrong with..."

"Me protecting my family? No, I don't."

"Forget it. I'm going to see Tanji." I went looking for the bag he brought with him from the hospital, finding it tucked in the back of the closet. "Keys in this pocket?" I asked, pulling the drawstring open before sticking my hand inside to find the pants he had on when he went in the hospital.

"KAPRI, DON'T..."

Instead of the Givenchy jeans, I grabbed his white tee, still stained with his blood from that day...that day...that day I almost... almost...almost lost...

"AAAAHHHHH! NOOOOO! ATIF!" Dropping the shirt to the floor, my eyes instinctively snapped shut, but it was too late. I couldn't get the image out of my head, it was burned in my brain...the stitches were real...his hair grew back but the stitches were real... "NOOOO!"

The room suddenly started spinning before everything went black. I felt a pair of hands catch me before I hit the floor...

# FIFTEEN
# TANJI

"How long do you think they're going to keep her?" I asked Prince as we rode to the hospital to visit Kapri. The doctors said she had a psychotic break one day after her visit from seeing Atif in a coma; she'd imagined that he came out of it and was being cared for in a home in Hoffman Estates. Meanwhile, she was still pregnant and they were worried about the baby. Although she wouldn't like it, it was probably best if she stayed in the mental institution either until he came out of the coma or until she had the baby, whichever came first.

We tried to keep her posted as best as we could with what was going on with him; I told her about his father coming from Armenia, she knew about Atif's mother visiting, and of course we kept her posted about his condition. What we didn't tell her was that the doctors were thinking about pulling the plug. Atif's father shut that down immediately. So did Free, his wife. Nobody knew they were married until Prince listened to the recording on his phone, and that shone a light on a lot of what was currently going on. She wanted to rekindle her relationship with her husband, quiet as it was kept. Atif's parents didn't seem to be too happy seeing her there at the hospital, but as long as she had that marriage certificate in her possession, there wasn't much they could do. The hospital staff honored that above anything else.

"Kapri ain't making a move without Atif, that's word. Long as he in a coma, she'll be under a doctor's care. Good thing Free finally gave the okay to have him moved to a private facility; at least they're in the same state."

"What about her brothers?"

"They good at Ma Dukes' crib. She talking about adopting them though, since they don't have any parents and their only living relative in the nuthouse..."

"Prince, don't say that about my friend."

He glanced over at me briefly before turning back to the road. "You right. My bad, baby." We rode along for a few miles, both somewhere lost in our own thoughts. "Aye, since we talking about stuff that we shouldn't say about Kapri, you stop talking about Monica being pregnant around her. We don't know if that's God's baby."

"She don't be paying me no attention," I reasoned.

"Any time somebody says anything about Atif, Hermes, or God, she turn her head. They could be talking about a belt. Could be talking about a purse. Hell, they could be praying. Just...just keep that to yourself until we find out what's what on that one."

"I will. What's killing me is that she ain't even showing, though. I don't think she even pregnant. Atif been in a coma for three months now. You'd think she'd have a baby bump or something, right?"

"Who? Kapri?"

"Naw. Monica."

Prince waved me off, focusing back on the road. "Ain't nobody worried 'bout that bird ass bitch," he scoffed, sucking his teeth. "We gotta take care of this business. Life goes on."

"Life goes on? I thought you and God were good friends."

"Fuck friends, Atif is my brother. I'm talking 'bout Monica being so pressed to be a part of the family."

"Either way, I just hope Kapri is okay." I sighed, staring out the window as we pulled up to the hospital. "She really is a good person."

"Yeah, I'm praying she makes it too."

---

I COULDN'T WAIT until things went back to what they were before the incident. Back when me and Prince snuck around the south side, back when Steve went and played G.I. Joe all over the country, back when side pieces knew their roles and played them to a T. Now it seemed as if everyone was on eggshells, tiptoeing around the inevitable. Every day I woke up, I had a strange feeling of dread. Somebody was about to die.

"Hey, Mr. Hermes," I greeted Atif's father with a hug. He'd been back and forth between two hospitals visiting with his son and future daughter-in-law, and it was beginning to show on his face. "How are you today?"

"Praying for good news on one of these two. I know my son loves this woman and she feels the same, so it's my duty to come and support her as well. That's what he would've wanted," he sighed.

"Have they given you an update on the baby?"

"The heartbeat is strong, and that's good," he smiled briefly, shoving his hands in his pockets. "They're giving her the vitamins for the baby through her IV and she's doing okay for now."

We both peeked in her room; my heart broke every time I came up here to see her staring blankly at the wall. That's all she did for the most part; she barely acknowledged our presence. The only time we saw some response from her was when someone mentioned Atif. Her head would turn slightly before she slipped back into a semi-comatose state. Now that was love. I couldn't imagine what I would do if something happened to Prince.

"How long do you think she'll..."

"Until she knows whether or not my son is okay," Atif's mother

Philomené interjected, kissing me on my cheek as I gave her a brief hug. "I know how she feels. Those Hermes men have that effect on you."

"Do we?" Atif's father wrapped his arm around her waist and she leaned into him, allowing him to be her strength.

"Yes, you do, my love. Your son moved me to Atlanta because mentally I couldn't handle living in the house you bought me. It reminded me too much of you."

"And now?" he questioned gently, moving her hair out of her face.

Smiling and blushing, she leaned in his ear to whisper her answer. He wrapped his arm around her just a little tighter; they reminded me so much of Atif and Kapri. Maybe there was some truth to Mama Hermes' words.

"I can't wait to meet my grandchild," she changed the subject. I loved Atif's mother. She was so full of life, bringing happiness and positivity every time she walked in a room. "We just need to keep the prayer warriors praying for all three of my babies."

My text ringer dinged, and I excused myself to check my phone. *Jealousy in the air tonight, I can tell,* I mused while reading Monica's message. Walking down the hall so I didn't interrupt the family's visit, I hit talk on her number to find out what she wanted.

"Tanji, can you come to my prenatal appointment with me? I still haven't heard nothing from God and the doctor say that we should be able to hear the baby's heartbeat today," she gushed.

I opened my mouth to give her an excuse, then changed my mind. "I'm in the middle of something right now, but yeah, I'll be there. Text me the information, okay?"

"Okay." she sounded excited that I'd be there, but I was on some other shit. I had to know more about this baby.

Monica was too fake in my opinion. On one hand, she would watch my kids for me with no problem, but she also carried too many bones for me. Monica was the one who told me about Steve and

Tangelica to begin with; even before Visa called me to verify my address. Monica confirmed Tangelica and Steve's alleged "engagement". Yeah, God mentioned it but I didn't believe him, and I found out by accident that Monica was the one who told her mother that Steve said Jenesis wasn't his child. It was time for me to start taking a few bones back myself.

## SIXTEEN
## PRINCE

We had too many discussions in front of Kapri, and Atif would be pissed if he knew how much stuff she really knew about. His father brought up Free and Atif's marriage while we were there and we chopped it up about that for a few minutes. He talked about looking into getting his son a divorce since they hadn't lived in the house with each other; the only thing they did was consummate their marriage before he left and came back to the city. Atif's parents were hoping Kapri gave birth to a boy in case...fuck it, I'm just gonna say it. In case Atif didn't come out of that coma.

"Who at the hospital with my son?" Atif's mother questioned, tapping me on my shoulder.

"We 'bout to head up that way now." I wiped my hand down my face and sighed. "Free up there. I didn't want to be in the same room with her while she..."

"Poisoning my son's mind," she finished. "I don't like her. She's wrong for my son and wrong for this family. Go up there and get that hoe bag away from my baby boy."

"Yes ma'am." I chuckled, looking around for Tanji. Atif used to crack on his mama all the time, as we all do, but at the end of the day, she wasn't the type of woman you crossed. "Tanji, come on!" I waved at her tucked off in a corner in the waiting room.

"Coming, babe." She jogged to where I was, wrapping her arm in mine. "Can you drop me off at the clinic?"

"For what, you pregnant?"

"No!" she yelled. "Monica..."

"Say less. Jus' gimme the address."

After I dropped her off, I went to meet up with AZ, who was our connect in everything else. AZ was a lawyer that had his own firm downtown with offices in the Hancock building, and he kept his shit on point. Not only did he have his hand in half the shit we had going on, he also knew how to get us out of it if we got caught. He was the one who ordered the hit on G Murda back in the day. Atif killed Hamm on his own because he didn't want the nigga to change his mind once he retired.

"What's goin' on, A?" We shook up before sitting down on the park bench overlooking the lake. "Tell me something good."

"First and foremost, what's goin' on wit' the God?" he questioned, rubbing his hands together.

"Still down, still nothing good."

"And wifey?"

"Going crazy." It was the truth.

"Armenia's biggest dope czar still here?"

"Unc still here."

"Y'all need to get God's wife away from him," he began. "I'm looking into how we can circumvent that marriage certificate of theirs, but you definitely need to get her from around him ASAP. No visits. Period."

"Is he aight now?"

"Lemme put it to you this way: God should already be back on the streets by now. Take that however you want to. I'll text you later." He stood up to adjust his tailored suit before dapping me up.

I sat back on the bench, watching the waves roll back and forth against the sand while pondering his words. AZ was that type of muthafucka who told you some shit and left you to think about what he said as opposed to just coming right out and saying it. If I was reading him right though, I needed to make Free an innocent victim of an unfortunate incident. As much shit as she instigated and sat back to watch her pawns do her business, I had no problem with being judge, jury and executioner on this one.

---

FREE JUMPED QUICKLY when she saw me walk into the ICU where God looked pale as ever. "I was speaking with my husband," she began.

"Get the fuck outta here, Free. Your little time is up."

"You know I'm being nice by allowing any of you to visit my husband, including his parents," she began, gathering her things. "One conversation with the chief physician and I'll be the only person here."

"You know, I'M being nice right now. One conversation with my pistol and you won't be talking to nobody," I growled.

"Don't find yourself in the same position that your brother is in," she whispered in my ear on her way to the door. Staring at Atif with a look on her face that was anything but wife-ish, she stepped back in the room to give him a quick peck on the cheek. "Leave the lipstick on his face for when his little girlfriend comes up here. I want her to see that her services are no longer needed."

"Beat it, bitch." I escorted her to the door and stood in her way when she tried to walk back in for a third time. She smirked quickly before walking towards the elevator, stabbing the buttons until it came. I gave her the finger as she crept on the elevator, heading back inside the room to wait on this one lil' nurse that used to give me pussy back in the day who coincidentally worked up here.

"I got that video you asked about." She walked in right behind me, handing me a flash drive. "Who is that lady?"

"Long story. Aye, how cool are you with the security people?"

"We good, why?"

"I need to know every time she come up here. If possible, I need for you an' ya' girls to have an excuse for her to not visit. Say y'all running tests, his blood pressure too high; say something."

"How much we gettin' paid?" She stuck her hand out, bobbing her head.

"Paid?" I slapped her hand with mine. "You can't hook ya' boy up off the love?"

"Prince, love don't live here! Not with yo' mama bringing your daughter and stepson up to the park to play with my kids, yelling to anybody who might be listening about how pretty her grandbabies are!"

*Damn, mama.* "How much you need?" I dug in my pocket, ready to give this girl everything I had on me if that's what it took.

"We'll take a thousand a piece," her eyes shone as she watched me peeling off hundred dollar bills.

"How many of y'all is it?"

"Ten."

"Ten? I only saw three of y'all at the desk!"

"You don't want her creeping up here on the night shift, do you?"

"Shit." I stopped counting, just handing her the whole knot. "Lemme know when those test results come back too."

"I got'chu, P," she cheesed, peeling off each bill slowly.

## SEVENTEEN
## ATIF

"She can't possibly love you as much as I do," Siranush's voice echoed through the darkness. "I need you, Atif. I NEED YOU. Why won't you love me? Huh? Why?" she wept.

I didn't want to love her. I wasn't interested in loving her. The woman who I wanted to love was here with me and that's all I needed. I mentally touched back on the day Kapri's words came to me clearer when I focused on tuning Siranush's constant nagging echo out. I heard her speaking with the nurse who came in from time to time and told me that I needed to pull through for my family. Nurse...Nurse...Damn, I can't remember her name, but I usually heard her either before my parents came or after.

Kapri begged me to let her stay. I remember her yelling, asking why she couldn't stay. I wanted her to stay; she needed to be here with me. That was the life I was looking forward to down in Miami. I needed my woman and my kids. Sometimes I saw her here, which I didn't understand. She should be taking care of my boys, visiting me every day, drinking water and taking her prenatal vitamins.

"God." I wondered why Prince had his war voice on. "I'm telling you this so you'll know. I'm killing your wife. Tonight."

This shit was whack as hell. I hated laying up in this void where I didn't know what was going on. I tried moving my fingers so he knew I was down for whatever he thought needed to be done, but just as they had since I got here, I couldn't.

"That bitch been giving you some medication to keep you in this coma. I don't know if she fucking the chief physician, but he said we not allowed to come visit you no more. She even got yo' mama on the fuckin' 'no contact' list. AZ working on a court order to make it look good, but I ain't waiting on that shit. I'm killing this bitch TONIGHT. Stay up, my nigga. We 'bout to get you back outchea real soon." He dapped me up before his voice faded.

"Where's Kapri?" I questioned the emptiness.

"I'm here, Atif," she called out from behind me. Her voice wasn't the echo like everyone else's since she was here with me. "What we doing today?"

"Kapri, you can't stay here," I began. "You gotta go."

"Why, Atif? I want to be with you. Why are you making me leave?"

"Did you know Free was my wife?"

"Yes."

"Do you know she trying to kill me?"

"She...what?"

"Kapri...baby, I want you to stay. I love you, girl. This whole thing is selfish. Selfish of me for asking you to stay and selfish of you for being here, knowing you pregnant. Where are you? Who taking care of my boys?"

"Atif..."

"Don't let Prince go after her alone. I know you ain't green out here, you my lady and you know what's what. Make sure he take care of that business on behalf of the family."

"Atif, will I ever see you again?" her voice wavered softly.

"I'm coming home, baby. I promise."

"I love you, Atif," she called out, moving away from me.

"I love you too," I responded, no longer feeling her presence.

The emptiness consumed me as it did when I first got here. I felt alone now; I knew she was gone. She never did tell me how she got here in the first place. I knew why I was here, but I was confused on how SHE was too. Didn't matter. What did matter was me getting the fuck up outta here. I'd been gone too long, it was time for me to remind these people why the streets called me GOD.

# EIGHTEEN
## KAPRI

Hearing voices discussing my husband, I turned to see an older man and woman sitting on the couch in my room as I blinked my surroundings clear. "I'm sorry, who are you?"

"Kapri?" The woman turned her head sharply towards me. "Let me get you a glass of water. I'm Atif's mother..."

"Philomené Boudreaux-Hermes," I wheezed, gulping down the cup of water that she held out in my direction. "Atif has told me so much about you."

"Call me mama, sweetie," she spoke with a gentle smile. "This is Atif's father, Aram Hermes." She waved him over with one hand while pouring me a second cup. Atif's father came and stood next to her with a fatherly grin. "How are you feeling, hun?"

I don't know what kind of water that was, but it felt good going down my throat. "I'm sorry we had to meet under these circumstances," I began before she stopped me.

"No, honey, no need to apologize. If nobody else understands what you're going through, I do. I married an Hermes man myself," she chuckled, patting my hand that I just noticed had an IV in it.

"Where am I?"

She looked to Atif's father to explain my current situation. "Sometimes people need a little extra help to cope with everyday life. When that happens, they bring them here," she tried to explain.

"I don't understand..."

"You're in an institution, Kapri. You went to visit my son in the hospital and the doctors said they found you in his room in the bed with him. When they tried to remove you, you began screaming that you weren't leaving, so they forcibly removed you and put you on a seventy-two-hour psych hold. When they felt like you needed more care than what they could give, they transferred you here," Atif's father kept it a hunnit with me, and for that I appreciated him.

"Where is Atif?"

"Still in the hospital, sweetie," she spoke. I shifted my gaze to her face and saw Atif all in her eyes.

*I'm coming home, baby. I promise...*Atif's words echoed in my head as I looked back and forth between both of his parents. "I need to get out of here." I looked around for the button to call the nurse.

"It's not that easy..." Atif's mother began.

"Mr. Hermes..." I wasn't trying to ignore her, but she wasn't giving me the responses I needed. "I know you know someone."

He slid his phone back in his pocket and stroked his beard. The twinkle in his eyes matched his son's brooding look. "Gimme ten minutes," he spoke bluntly.

"Aram..."

"She's my son's wife, Philomené. She needs to be with him," he respectfully cut her off, pushing the button to get the nurse, who tapped briefly on the door before entering. "Miss, get this stuff off of her immediately."

"Sir, the doctor has to come..."

"NOW, DAMMIT!"

The nurse jumped and moved quickly as possible to remove the IV from my arm, taking the stint out of the crook of my elbow's crease with medical precision. "Is there anything else you require, sir?"

"Get her clothes. Have the doctor here with her release papers by the time she's dressed," he dismissed her with a wave of his hand. The nurse hurried anxiously out of my room, closing the door tightly behind her.

"Mr. Hermes, I understand there's some confusion about our policies and procedures," the doctor barged in the room arrogantly, "but your daughter..."

"Don't insult me by insinuating my ignorance of your policies," Atif's father stopped the doctor in mid-sentence. "I don't give a fuck about your procedures when you have one of mine in here. Produce some release paperwork for my daughter in the next ten seconds or find out who you're dealing with. See, we're not the type of family that you're obviously accustomed to talking down to; I'll have your throat slit by the time you get to the nurse's station. Are we both on the same page now, doc?" he sneered.

"Maybe security can help you understand my position," the doctor smirked cockily as he headed to the door, adjusting his wire frames.

"And maybe your wife Melissa can help you understand mine." Atif's father pulled up a video of a woman bound and gagged on his phone, flashing it in the doctor's eyesight. "Clock's still ticking."

"You...you can't..." the doctor stuttered.

"Hospital security only protects YOU. How well do you trust your local precinct?"

"Lemme make sure we have paper in the printer," he scurried into the hallway. Yeah, this was definitely Atif's father.

"Ready to see your husband, Kapri?" Philomené cheesed in my direction as I texted Tanji, letting her know I was leaving the hospital. I signed the discharge papers that the doctor tossed on the table before rushing back out the room to call his wife.

"Yes, mama." I heard the confidence return to my own voice. "I'm ready."

# NINETEEN

# TANJI

"Monica Houston, the doctor will see you now," the nurse called us back to the examining room. I got there just in time; the nurse quickly took her weight and blood pressure before leaving the hospital gown on the exam table with the thin sheet to cover up with. "She'll be with you shortly."

"I didn't get a chance to thank you for coming with me today." Monica undressed from the waist down, keeping on her tank top. "I can't believe God is such a deadbeat."

"Are you sure this his baby?" I just came right out and asked. Monica told anybody that would listen that God was her baby fahva; even the mailman was asking people if it was true.

"Yeah, I'm sure. I ain't out here having sex with everybody else's man; I know who my child's father is!" She lowkey tried my life.

"Oh, okay. You say you ain't out here bad, but God got a woman though." I crushed her soul with those words. "That he ape shit in love with, too."

"I'on care," she mumbled lowly. "He gon' take care of my baby whether he in love or not."

The doctor came in, all smiles. "Ahhh, Mrs. Houston. How are we today?"

"MRS. Houston? Don't you mean Ms. Houston? I'm the one that's married into the family," I spoke up.

"No, the paperwork clearly says Mrs." The doctor double-checked Monica's chart. "Husband not listed because he's a celebrity and this is a 'love' child?"

I burst into laughter. This bitch can't be serious. THIS BITCH CAN'T BE SERIOUS...MY CHEST... "Oh, my GOD," I cackled. She was carrying a love child, alright: sweet baby Jesus. "I...I must've forgot about that. Yeah, yeah, she carrying a 'love' baby." I air quoted.

"Can we please continue?" Monica hissed in my direction, lifting her gown so the doctor could squeeze the gel on her stomach.

"Like I was saying before, Mrs. Houston, I don't think we'll find..." she spoke with concern.

"Can you please just check? I know my baby wants her mama to hear her heartbeat," she insisted.

*Aw hell.* "Wait..."

"Can I speak with you out in the hallway, Mrs. Houston?" The doctor nodded her head towards the door, squinting back and forth between me and Monica.

"Who, me?"

"Yes."

"Umm...sure." I stood up, grabbing my purse and cautiously creeping out the door behind her. "What's wrong with the baby?"

"That's the thing," she whispered. "There is no baby."

"No baby? Why are we here then?"

"Because your sister..."

"In-law. My sister-in-law."

"Your sister-in-law has it in her head that there is," she continued. "She's suffering from pseudocyesis, which is when the body displays all the symptoms of pregnancy, but the patient isn't actually pregnant."

"What! How?"

"We aren't sure exactly how..." The doctor looked back and forth between me and the door, "but she came in and she had all the symptoms. When we did a pregnancy test, there were no hormones in her urine nor her blood, so we did an ultrasound. We didn't find an embryo."

"Well, what the hell y'all expect me to do? Y'all the professionals. Slap some sense into her!"

"We can't do that, Mrs. Houston. After all, we did take an oath to first do no harm. But as someone who she seems to have a bond with..."

"Tuh, I got my own problems," I uttered, walking back in the room. "Monica! Stop wasting these people time faking this fucking pregnancy! Put yo' clothes on and come on!"

"First God abandons me, now you let this bitch trick you into believing I ain't pregnant! I'm NOT leaving until I hear my baby's heartbeat!" she screamed. "DOCTOR! DO YOUR FUCKING JOB!"

"Girl, bye." I tucked my purse under my arm and left her with the doctor. Let them figure that out.

Digging in my purse for my phone, I found it and was just about to order a ride on the Lyft app when I noticed I had a missed notification. "Prince better...wait...Kapri?" Hitting her number, I sat down in the waiting room with my left leg jumping, waiting for her to pick up.

"Tanji?"

"BIIIIIITCH!" I yelled before I knew it. The receptionist came from behind her desk and escorted me out mid scream. "When you wake up! Me and Prince 'bout to come up there!"

"Nah, meet me up here at the hospital where Atif is. Me and Mama 'bout to walk in here now," she expressed.

"I thought ol' girl said we couldn't visit?"

"Tif's lawyer got an injunction; Salty Bae ain't stopping shit round here," she giggled. "I'm walking in now. Girl, yo' man here, you might as well slide through."

"Oh, so y'all just having a little kickback in Atif's room, huh?" I snickered.

"Baby need all the love he can get right now. I been gone too long. I'll see you in a minute."

"On my way, sis." Calling a Lyft, I sat in the back seat and huffed loudly until the driver sped up and dropped me off. Hurrying inside the facility, I gave them my information and got a visitor's pass. They would only let two visitors go in his room at a time because of his condition, but the whole family was out in the hallway waiting for their turn. I hugged Atif's father as Prince wrapped his arm around my waist, and they went back to talking to a big man built like a football player dressed impeccably in a tailored suit.

Peeking through the glass, I smiled seeing Kapri looking semi healthy sitting next to Atif's mother, holding her hand. Both women had their eyes closed; Atif's mother was speaking while Kapri nodded with tears streaming from her eyes. "That's right, sis. Pray your love back," I whispered. As I watched, I saw...wait...did his hand just move? "Prince..."

"So, when the judge came in and saw me, you already know..." the retired football player lookalike was telling a story that had my man and Atif's father mesmerized.

"Prince..." I couldn't tear my eyes away from Atif's hand reaching out for Kapri in slow motion. With her eyes still closed, she didn't even know what was happening. I tried tapping him on his shoulder, but he moved away from me.

"...all he could say was 'granted' before banging that gavel! Tif's wife was PISSED!" they laughed together.

"ZADRIAN!"

"What, Tanji?" he yelled.

I pointed towards the room where Atif gently placed his hand on Kapri's baby bump. Opening her eyes slowly, she looked down in shock as his eyes popped open....

## TWENTY

# PRINCE

Two doctors and three nurses pushed past us, rushing to Atif's room as Kapri held his hand and stroked his arm. Atif's mother pulled her away from him gently so his medical team could check his responses, but from where I stood, the God was back.

His girl and his mother were in the room when the doctor removed the tubes from his throat. Something in the back of my mind told me some kind of way his father would end up in that room too. Hearing water running behind me, I saw Unc with the mask over his face and the long gown that we had to wear to minimize any outside germs already on. Me and AZ moved out of his way, watching him boldly walk in the room as if he was about to add his professional opinion to his son's diagnosis.

"What was she giving him?" AZ questioned, watching the scene unfold in front of him with a hard stare as Kapri cried. I pulled Tanji just a little closer to me, since she was already sniffing loudly off to my side.

"Propofol."

"You know she could've got her hands on that shit any kind of way. All she had to do was respond to an ad; you can get better dope on the dark web than you can get in the streets."

"Aye, don't say that shit too loud; we'll all be out of work outchea," I snickered, dapping him up. "We ain't getting them Trump deals, skin too dark."

"That's facts," AZ shook up with me a second time. "Tell the God I'll be up here to check him out later, I don't wanna interrupt the moment."

"No doubt," I nodded in his direction before he headed towards the elevator.

"Prince," Kapri stepped out of Atif's room with red eyes and a huge smile on her face, followed by his mother. "Baby wants to talk to you."

I started preparing to go in when she grabbed my arm as Tanji and Mrs. Hermes walked off down the hall. "Is Free still alive?"

"For now."

"I'm going too."

"What you—"

"You know what I'm talking about. Talk to 'Tif," she whispered before joining her mother-in-law. "Don't be trying to talk him to death either, Prince! Y'all got time!"

"Whaddup my G." I walked in and went to dap him up. "Welcome home."

"Thanks man," he responded hoarsely. "What's going on with Free?"

"She still out here for now."

"Wasn't you..." he paused for a second, trying to rub his throat, "... wasn't you supposed to?"

"Had another issue come up with Monica."

"Monica who?"

"That one bitch you used to fuck with."

"Wha..." he pointed at the cup of water on the table near him. I passed it to him, he took a few sips before sitting the cup down next to the pitcher. "...what about her?"

"Bitch busted out all my windows and flattened my tires on my shit looking for you! You know I tried to kill that hoe," we chuckled together.

"Fuck she looking for me for?" he questioned.

"She say she pregnant by you, but me personally I think she faking it."

"Pregnant by me, huh? Everybody jus' wanna fuck the God..." he wheezed, taking another sip of his drink. "...now that I ain' fuckin' wit' these bitches, I go from lukewarm to hot. Bitch ain't pregnant by me," he snickered.

"She ain't pregnant by nobody, bitch ain't even showing. Even Kapri got a lil' bump."

"Find her ass and tell her nah, I'm good love, enjoy," he snickered. "I heard these nurses say that shit once when they came in here."

"Aye, speaking of Kapri, what she talking about?"

God got quiet for a second, staring off into nothing for a few seconds before he spoke. "She want to go put in work, but hell naw. She pregnant."

"Man, I thought we was gonna have to check her back in that institution."

"Institution? What you talking about?"

*Damn, I didn't mean to say that.* "She went a little crazy with you being in a coma, so the doctors checked her into a lil' spot until she got her mind right."

"When she get out?"

"She woke up a few hours ago. Pop got her paperwork rushed and she came straight here."

"Take her to the house and leave her ass there. Better yet, take her to yo' mama house so she think she bout to go, but leave her ass there." He stroked his beard for a few seconds, then slapped the cup off the table.

"A'ight, G. You got your phone?" I stood up and got ready to leave. God wasn't paying me no attention; knowing his woman went crazy with him gone was doing something to him. I could tell by the look on his face. "I'll get up with you later, G." Checking for my phone, I nodded in his direction and left.

---

SITTING in the parking structure waiting on this bitch to come back outside was boring as fuck, but it had to be done. I got a text from Jeff that they robbed some niggas at one of her trap houses, and she was about to run out there to see what was going on. Now this chick had a personal assistant, PLUS a right hand man that was fucking around with Gabrielle before we killed her, yet she was going out here to check her own traps. You can't find good help nowhere these days.

Free finally came out dressed in all black and some heels and hopped in her black Bentley. Following her as she wheeled through the streets of Milwaukee, I sent Jeff a text to get the goons ready as I blew through a red light with my pistol on my lap. I heard the sirens right before the red and blue lights hopped behind me.

Tucking my piece in the fake secret compartment underneath my seat, I grabbed my driver's license from my pocket as they walked up.

"What's the rush?" the white cop questioned.

"Just got a text that the wife at home fucking somebody on my couch," I lied. "Hard as I work every night and this what she do with her free time? Sicka this shit, man!" I yelled, punching the steering wheel to make it look good. If we was in the city, I wouldn't have a problem, but I'm in a whole other state. I wasn't trying to get locked up in no damn Wisconsin; what would be a red-light ticket in the Chi might get me five years out here.

"Calm down, son. You don't want to do anything you might regret in the heat of the moment," the older black officer counseled. "Where do you live?"

I gave him the address to Free's trap house; since it didn't look like I could shoot her tonight, I could at least get her caught up. I got a police escort to the front door. They were halfway down the block when the shooting started. I ducked quick, pulling out my phone to send God and AZ a text that this nigga Jeff set me up before I heard a loud BOOM and flames erupted all around me.

# TWENTY-ONE

## FREE

I told my father that Aram Hermes wasn't the great warrior that had everyone in our village of Ararat hanging on his every word. There was nothing honorable about a man that Interpol knew as *Karich* (scorpion). With all that being said, had Aram kept his word in the old country and kept our secret, his son would love me, AND WE COULD'VE LIVED HAPPILY EVER AFTER. Certainly, we wouldn't be here.

Growing up, I can admit that I wasn't the belle of our village. Constantly teased by the other children, I looked forward to the day when I would be the swan and not the ugly duckling. My father always told me I was the most beautiful girl in the world, and when I got older my Prince Charming would sweep me off my feet.

Atif's father Aram was the most feared man in our village, and the most respected. My father, who was a low-level hustler where we were from, told us the story about him saving Aram from a lifetime behind bars the day he was arrested. According to my father, he was there when the police were in the middle of raiding a house full of drugs and weapons that Aram just walked up to when he ran over and told them that he owned the home. Aram told the police that he had the wrong address and showed them a piece of paper with the address of a house across the street. The police knew he was lying, but since both men stuck to their story and they couldn't prove otherwise, my father ended up in prison.

Once I got older, he told me about Atif being my Prince Charming and how bright my future would be. Although I'd never met him because he grew up here in the states, I saw pictures sent to me by my sister who lived in the U.S. I was looking forward to getting to know him when Aram came back to Armenia, but he told us that Atif stayed behind with his mother. When I heard he would be coming for the wedding, I was excited. My neighbor gave me her old wedding dress, and everyone in our village chipped in for a small reception to be held near the Hermes estate that sat at the edge of our village. I might be ugly, but I swear I was worth it. After all, Atif Hermes was about to be my husband.

The night before he was supposed to come, Aram came to my mother's home to visit. He told us Atif knew nothing about the arrangement, but he would speak to him and everything would be okay. After handing my mother more money than she'd seen in the past five years, he motioned for me to follow him outside, so we could talk about what he called 'family business'. Once we got outside, he asked me if I was a virgin. Of course I was; his son would be the first and only man that I'd ever wanted to be with. I fantasized about my wedding night with Atif every night. His father snapped his fingers, and two men came from nowhere and raped me. All the while I was screaming for him to help me, he stood off to the side smoking a cigar and watched, telling me that his son needed a woman with experience.

That situation broke me, but I still gathered myself up once they were done and got cleaned up. The next day I put on a smile and married his son, to his disdain. On our wedding night when we consummated our marriage, Atif put a sheet over my face before he entered me. That hurt my heart, yet knowing that he was still my husband I didn't care if I had to wear that sheet for the rest of our union. Finding out I wasn't pure, he rejected me, although I tried to explain what happened the day before. His father lied and told him that he found out a few hours before that I was the village whore, and they had security escort me to the front gate of their estate in the middle of the night wrapped in only a sheet.

Aram suddenly remembered his promise to my father and started negotiating an Armenian mob to run the streets of Chicago. In exchange for my silence about the incident that happened on the eve of what should've been the best day of my life, he vowed that once Atif established his rule over Chicago, he would tell him about what happened, and we would run the city together. I would have money to send home to my family and although we couldn't get my father out of prison, he would at least be comfortable. My niece Eisha knew two girls from our village who were eager to get to the states and work for Aram, so Atif took them back with him.

Meghranush was my best friend growing up, and we kept in touch. She told me about Atif changing her name to Gabrielle and to call him God. Kayiane, aka Michaela, never liked me, and was upset when she found out that Atif and I were married. Her intent was to be Mrs. Hermes, so she thought she was going to get closer to him and convince him to divorce me. Then when Kayiane told me about this girlfriend of his and neither one of us could have him only added to my pain. Hence the reason I punched her in the stomach that day in her apartment, and while she was bent over, inserted an empty needle in her neck, filling her vein with air. Before her body dropped, my men strung her up from the rafters and made it look like a suicide. I typed the suicide note on her iPad with her cold, dead fingers after I wiped it down, and dropped it directly under her body. They didn't even investigate her death.

Never did I tell Eisha about what happened to me; I only shared with her the good times Atif and I had for those couple of hours. It didn't sit well with me that she wanted to harm him over that mob thing; Atif gave me the best time of my life, and I was looking forward to spending the rest of my days as a Hermes woman. She was looking forward to running the Armenian mob in the city and was determined to hold Atif to his word. When we found out about Meghranush, I was upset because I never got to say goodbye. That was part of the reason I started a war with my husband, but the biggest reason was because he refused to love me based on his father's words.

That day I saw Aram Hermes and his wife at the hospital burned me up inside. Love oozed off of them, and seeing them standing side by side, I saw my husband. Knowing he was the sole reason for my angst, I hated him. Nuritsa told me about Atif's girlfriend, and that's who I was prepared to have words with. Since Atif never bothered to divorce me, I used our marriage out of spite in order to piss his father off. I had no issue with Atif's mother, but since she was still crazy in love, she was an enemy of mine by default. I had EVERYONE banned from visiting him just by waving around our marriage certificate and used that as my chance to tell Atif how I felt about him and what his father did. I knew he could hear me while in that coma, he had no other choice but to listen to my feelings.

I didn't tell anyone, but Atif came out of that coma about a month and a half ago while I was there. After I poured my heart out to him, he asked me where was Kaplan, Karen...what was her name? Kapi? Wait...Kapri. The woman's name that he was moaning right before he woke up. I first saw his manhood rise slightly before he opened his eyes, then when he saw me he frowned up.

"*Fuck is you doing here?*" *he spat, blinking at his surroundings.* "*Where's Kapri?*"

"*Welcome home, love.*" *I dabbed at the sweat on his brow.* "*It's good to see you. Why do you keep blinking, is there something wrong with your eyes?*"

"*I'm trying to blink your ugly ass gone, but it ain't working. Get the fuck out of my room, Siran!*"

"*Oh, I'm ugly, huh?*" *I chuckled bitterly, going for my purse. My original plan was to give Aram a shot of Propofol while he wasn't looking and kill his ass, but keeping his one and only child, his pride and joy in a coma wasn't a bad idea either. I slipped the needle in his IV so quick that he didn't know what hit him until that drug hit his system. "You can come out the coma when you decide to be a husband and not an asshole."*

Prince wanted to move Atif from the hospital to a facility, and I gave the okay because the hospital was too efficient; they'd started running tests on his blood and it was only a matter of time before they knew. I didn't see Aram without his estranged wife after that, and she rolled her eyes at me every time. They didn't know that every time I saw them I smiled, knowing I had their son's life in my purse.

What nobody knew was that Jeff was my right hand man; he'd infiltrated Atif's operation while Meghranush was still alive. I didn't know everything about what he was doing, but with Jeff there as my eyes and ears I knew enough. Prince's family wasn't from our village, however since he and Atif were so close, he was on my shit list too. I promised Jeff the city of Chicago and Milwaukee too as far as I was concerned if he could get rid of Prince. Judging from the explosion in front of one of my trap houses that put a smile on my face, it looked like Jeff was about to be the King of the Chi.

"Did I do good, Free?" Jeff was sitting on my right side; we watched the flames from Prince's truck dance high in the air.

"You did good, Jeff. You did real good," I nodded happily. Starting up the car, we pulled off the block to discuss strategy; after all, with Prince gone and Atif still in the hospital, he would need a new right hand. Jeff was the perfect person to slide in that position. Phase three of the Hermes family divide and conquer plan was in full effect.

"I got my man back...I got my man back," I sang to myself standing in Prince's mother's bathroom. At first, I was upset that Prince left me at his mother's house and I couldn't do what Atif asked of me while we were in the dark place. But spending that time with my little brothers reminded me that I needed to be surrounded by family, not out in the streets four months pregnant. Jacari and Jacoby were getting better by the day, and they were excited to be welcoming their nephew in a few months. Atif and I discussed the fact that we would have to tell Jacoby the truth at some point, but at his young age that wouldn't be anytime soon.

Prince's mother was nice; my brothers stopped calling her ma'am a while back, referring to her as Auntie V. She was sweet towards me too; making sure I had more than enough food, checking that I took my prenatal vitamins that day, and giving me the biggest bed at her home. We talked for a while, and she told me that Atif gave her money every other day, so I didn't need to worry about whether or not she was okay. Even with him being in the hospital, she still had more than enough because her son picked up where he left off.

Me and Tanji made plans to work out in the morning and go

shopping the next day. My snap back game had to be strong; I wasn't going to lift weights, but I was going to hit the treadmill and bikes for a few hours. Atif would kill me if he found out I walked into anyone's gym in the first place.

Seeing something blinking on my side, I saw my phone was ringing off the hook with a phone number that hadn't been saved in my phone. I was a little leery of seeing who it was, after all it could've been Free. I was in such a good head space and didn't need anyone to mess that up. Then again, it could've been Atif, so I answered it.

"Kapri?" a male voice boomed in my ear.

"Yes?" I replied.

"Kapri, this is AZ, Atif's lawyer. You seen Prince?"

"No, why?"

"You got his girl phone number?"

"AZ, right?"

"Yeah."

"I can't just give you her number like that considering that I don't know you. What's wrong?"

He sighed hard in my ear before he spoke. "I understand that, Kapri, but this is important. I need ol' girl number, trying to see if she know where he at."

"Oh, I know where he at. He left me at his mama house and went to Milwaukee."

"Shit, shit, SHIT!" he yelled. I heard a loud bang and the phone hung up.

*What was that all about?* I wondered, turning my ringer back on. A second number called me that wasn't saved, and I took a deep breath to try and shake the eerie chill that settled in my spirit. "Hello?"

"Kapri, let me apologize for hanging up on you. That was rude and disrespectful, I shouldn't have done that. Second, call your father-in-law and tell him to check Atif's phone. Then have him call me at this number, a'ight?" AZ spoke pointedly.

"Okay. Is everything okay?"

"I wish I could say yeah, but the truth is no. Everything is fucked up. We'll talk more soon, okay?" His voice calmed down some, however I could tell he was still tight about whatever was going on.

"Okay." I hung up with him and called Papa Hermes, delivering the message. Thanking me, he asked how I was doing and told me he'd see me tomorrow. I went to check on my brothers and talk to Prince's mother for a little while when we heard banging on the front door. Seeing her go for her gun before answering the door at such a late hour, I grabbed a knife from the kitchen, tucking it in my pocket before running behind her. She threw the door open and Tanji was standing there in tears, her car still running and parked crookedly in the middle of the street with the driver's side door wide open.

"Tanji? What's wrong?"

"HE'S DEAD! KAPRI THEY SAID HE'S DEAD!" she screamed, collapsing in Prince's mother's arms.

"Who's dead, Tanji? Atif?" my hands shook as I waited for her answer.

"NO!" she sobbed uncontrollably. Prince's mother let her go, waiting anxiously for her next words.

"Who's dead, Tanjalyn?"

"Pr...Pri...ZADRIAN!"

"My son?" she clutched her chest, backing away from the door. "My son is gone?"

"AZ...AZ came..." both women broke down and cried together.

My mind touched back on my last phone call. *AZ called...AZ called me first...*Tanji's biggest fear came true; Prince got caught up in some street beef and lost his life behind it. Technically she was still grieving her husband; Steve's death was only a few months ago. No matter how she felt about him those last few weeks, it didn't change the fact that they had been together since high school and had a child together. Is this what I had to look forward to: crying in Atif's mother's arms because he was gone? Maybe Tanji had a valid point.

"Is there anything I can do for you ladies?" I convinced them both back in the house and led them to the living room. They both shook their heads as I grabbed two cups of water from the kitchen.

Free was officially on my shit list. I had a feeling Atif told Prince to leave me here, but that was before this happened. Something told me that she had something to do with Atif being in a coma for as long as he was, but I had no proof. My husband kicked my own mother off a pier because of how shitty of a parent she was. Watching Tanji and Prince's mother as they grieved the loss of a great man, I knew it was time for me to return the favor.

I COULD NOT BREATHE. AZ came to our condominium downtown to give me the horrible...oh my God. *He's gone...My Prince is gone...*" NOOOO!!"

"Tanji, lemme take you somewhere," Kapri soothed, finally calming Prince's mother down as best as she could. "Where do you want to go?"

"I'm coming," I grabbed my purse and phone, tossing her my keys. "I know where I wanna go, too," I sniffed.

"Where we going?"

"Take me down to Chinatown and throw me off the overpass so I can be with my man," I sobbed.

"Tanji..."

"PRINCE! WHYYYY!"

"Sweetie, you got babies to think about. I can't do that," she spoke softly as we pulled away from the curb.

"Please, Kapri! I'd do it for you. I swear I'd do it for you..."

"Listen, sis. I'm going up to Milwaukee to dead that bitch Free once and for all. She won't be looking for me or you to come after her, if anything she'll be looking for a man. We just need to find out where she be and lay her ass down," she growled.

"Kapri...what?"

"Check it, Atif got a room in the house where he keeps all these guns and pistols, exclusive shit that ain't nowhere on the streets. We go up there, get friendly with some people, find out where the good dope at, and I guarantee it'll lead back to her some kind of way," she schooled. "Get in good with her and right when she get comfortable... BAM!" She made me jump. "Make that bitch head explode like a pumpkin."

"Atif ain't gonna..." I wiped my eyes, staring at her strangely.

"I'm sicka y'all talking about what Atif gonna do," she grumbled. "Free walking the world the epitome of her name, meanwhile my baby in the hospital, Michaela hung herself, and my brother just got killed. Way I see it, we losing. We gotta take the W at some point."

The more I thought about it, the more it made sense in a crazy way. Kapri sounded like she put some thought into this plan of hers, and I wanted in to avenge my baby's death. Free was the reason that I now had to explain to both of my babies that their daddy was in heaven, looking down on their every move. It would make me feel a lot better if I could at least throw in the fact that her ass was in hell. "I'm in, sis. What we gotta do?"

"Tomorrow instead of going shopping, we hit the gun range," she smiled maniacally.

---

"IT'S YOU," I walked around in the emptiness of our condo, talking to the man who showed me what love really was. "Every single time, it's you, Zadrian. I want to hold you in my hands as my lips brush against the softness of your chest, my love." Touching the back of the couch where we snuck and made love the first night me and the kids moved in, I felt his spirit. The tears stung hotly against my cheeks; I just wanted to hold him in my arms one more time, feel his breath as his chest rose and contracted underneath my palm. "I know you don't need me Zadrian, but you want me, and I want you...I want you, Zadrian."

I opened the doors to the balcony and stood watching the sun rise over Lake Michigan, the ever-moving waves served as a metaphor to my unyielding pain. "Zadrian...there's nothing in this world that will stop me from choosing you every night before I fall asleep, every morning when I wake up I promise I'll choose you. Always..." Sitting in his chair on the balcony, I reminisced on the last time we slow danced together out here. Afterwards, I sat on his lap and Zadrian held me close, whispering in my ear all the reasons why he loved me and why I was the one for him. We talked about our future, our future with our babies. Zadrian and I were supposed to go down to the place this week to start the process for him to adopt Stevie Jr., plus he wanted another son. I wanted so badly to give him a boy.

The wind kissing the back of my neck was what broke my train of thought. I realized I was standing on top of the table with one foot over the railing.

"Mommy?" Jenesis called sleepily from inside the apartment. "I'm hungry."

Taking a deep breath, I balanced myself and calmly stepped down from the table top. Zadrian would never forgive me if I went through with what my body pleaded. I longed to be free of this world and be with the man I should have married, but like Kapri said, I had babies to think about. What would happen to them if I was no longer around? They needed me as much as I needed their father.

"Zadrian, my love, I promise I won't let Free get away with taking you away from me. I promise."

"Where's Daddy?" my baby girl rubbed her eyes and questioned innocently. "He wasn't in his bed." How can I look at her staring at me with Zadrian's eyes and tell her that her daddy is now her angel?

"Come here, princess," I called her by the nickname her daddy...*oh my God, why?* Sniffing, I collected my thoughts as I rubbed her hair. "Remember when I told you that your daddy Steve was in heaven with the angels?"

"No Mommy, MY daddy. Not Stevie's daddy, MINE," she inquired sweetly.

"Yes princess, your daddy," I wiped the tears as they streamed down my face. "Your daddy has gone to heaven with Stevie's daddy."

"But why, mommy?" her grey orbs saturated with sadness, smashing my heart to pieces yet again. "He doesn't love me?"

"Princess, daddy loves you more than everything in this world," I began. "But right now...right now God needed him to be one of his angels to watch over you, pretty girl," my voice warbled.

"Mommy I need Uncle God's phone number. He can't keep my daddy," she went in our bedroom and pulled my phone from my purse. "Can you call him and tell him I need for my daddy to come home?" her bottom lip shook as her eyes shone.

"Jenesis...baby..." I pulled her close to me, hugging her tightly when the floodgates burst wide open. If only it were that easy, if heaven had a phone I would call him and demand that he come home... "ZADRIAN!"

My phone rang as my baby hugged me tightly, begging me to call Atif and make him send her daddy home.

"Tanji, we gotta be at the range early before they get crowded. The one in Des Plaines open at 9 and you still gotta drop the kids off."

"Lemme get Stevie up and I'll meet you at mama's, okay?" I went to the bathroom to wash my face before waking up my son.

"I'm already dressed, and Mama cooked, so hurry up."

"I'm gonna have Grammy call Uncle God so my daddy can come home," Jenesis huffed before wiping her face and stomping off to her bedroom, slamming the door. Prince left me with a piece of him in his baby; that girl was just like her daddy.

# TWENTY-FOUR

# ATIF

"Pop, that can't be right," I spoke as my father explained to me for the seventh time that Prince was in an explosion and didn't make it out alive. "Did you see his body?"

"The coroner sent me this pic," he spoke solemnly, showing me the picture on his Android. Prince was still clutching his phone in his hand, the same phone that he used to send me the text letting me know that nigga Jeff was a snake. "Atif..."

"Get me outta here, Pop," I spoke calmly.

My mother moved closer to where I was, resting her hand on mine. "Son, your body needs to heal..."

"Ma, I'm good," I cut her off. "Get me outta here, Pop."

"Son..." Out of both of them, Pop knew what was going on in my head.

"POP GET ME THE FUCK OUTTA HERE!" I slapped the lamp off the stand next to me, glaring at him ferociously.

"Son, let the doctors come and examine you, then we'll go from there," he reiterated sternly.

Prince was dead, Michaela was dead, and Free was knocking off my whole squad because she was a woman scorned. What happened to the good old days when bitches keyed your car, called ya girl to argue about which one of them you fucked better, and cried on the couch while watching rom coms and eating a gallon of ice cream? These new age bitches was too much; busting pistols, ordering hits, and trying to be the king. There was only one me. Wife or not, Free brought this on herself.

———

THE DOCTORS RELEASED ME, but with restrictions. They thought I would have some memory loss but spending three months in a coma gave my brain the extra time it needed to fully heal from the blow to my skull. I was on a cane and had limited mobility; they said I was only about 75% back to what I was before the incident. As long as I wasn't laid up in a hospital room, I could heal myself. I knew me a lot better than those muthafuckin' doctors anyway.

I was back at the crib, and Ma Dukes was here with me. Kapri had been moving funny the past few weeks, and when I asked her about what she had going on, she told me she was spending time with Tanji helping her with the kids. Prince left everything he owned to his daughter; with that money plus what she got from the military every month, baby girl was a multi-millionaire.

At six in the morning, Kapri should be poking her booty out and letting a real G get some early morning pussy. Instead she was in the shower singing Hit 'Em Up by Tupac at the top of her lungs. I guess she must've forgot I was here:

> *First off, fuck you bitch and the click you claim*
> *West side, when we ride come equipped with game*

"Atif, turn that music down!" my mother ran in our bedroom still wrapping her robe around her. "You're gonna wake up the kids!"

"Ma, that's not me, that's ya daughter-in-law," I pointed to the bathroom door. My mother tiptoed to the door and stood quietly for a few seconds while Kapri cussed the house down.

*Grab ya glocks when you see Kapri*
*Call the cops, don't wanna fuck with me*
*Who shot me, but you bitches didn't finish*
*Now you bout to feel the wrath of a menace*
*Bitch, I hit you UP*

"See, this is all you and your father's doing," she pointed at me, squinting her eyes. "This is what happens when your husband calls himself 'God' and your father-in-law is on a first name basis with law enforcement agencies on three continents. I'll deal with you both later," she spat venomously. "KAPRI! OPEN THE DOOR SWEETHEART, IT'S MAMA!" she called out loudly.

"Hey mama," Kapri appeared at the door, all smiles. "I'm sorry, did I wake you?"

"Yes, sweetie," my future wife had my whole family in the palm of her hand. Mama's expression changed with the quickness as she stood stroking her shoulder. "Is everything okay?"

"Everything's GREAT!" she cheesed.

Staring her up and down, I hoped whatever excuse she gave my mother was believable because I was about to fuck something. Yeah, everything was great, a'ight. Once I opened that pussy up, everything would be fantastic, and she'll be back snoring; I just needed about thirty good, peaceful minutes.

"Okay, baby. I know you're grown and this your house now, but can you turn the music down a little? You gonna wake the kids up," she whispered. Footsteps and a quick knock on my bedroom door had me grabbing my cane as the door squeaked open.

"Is everything a'ight in here?" my father questioned. This nigga ain't have his shirt on; I know they ain't in here fucking in my house. Especially since I couldn't when I was growing up.

"Bye y'all," I put my cane back and waved them both out of my room. You can't talk shit to your parents, but you can put their asses out of your bedroom. "Ma, cook me some breakfast."

"Tuh, you got a wife." She smirked as my father wrapped his arm around her waist before they disappeared through the door.

"Yeah Atif, you got a wife." Kapri smirked, rubbing her lemon and coconut oil mix on her baby bump. My son jumped at her touch; I was jealous because they played tag all day and I couldn't join in.

"Come over here and let me taste that pussy juice on my lips." I stood up and helped her rub oil on her back. "Let me make you my little strawberry shortcake," I moaned in her ear.

"Mmm," she moaned, dropping to her knees. I pulled her up quickly; as much as I wanted her to swallow my meat, she was still pregnant. Oh, but once she drop that load, I'm skeeting all in her face daily. "Let's role play. I'll be Burger King and you can be McDonald's. I'll have it my way and you'll be loving it," her silly ass uttered.

I stuck two fingers in her gushy with my tongue down her throat. Her pussy was TOO wet; I was trying to find out what she was up to and she was tricking me with that puss. "That's not a bad idea, babe. Your shit too wet though, you dripping off my fingertips," I whispered in her ear. "Lil' pussy got some power this morning, don't it?"

"Lil' pussy always got some power, got me full of your baby didn't it," she bit her bottom lip with her eyelids low. "Got her so hot that girl thumpin'. Feel it again, 'Tif."

I slid two fingers back in her slit with my dumb ass, what I do that for? Leading her to the bed, I bent her over and arched that back, sliding balls deep in her guts. Sticking those same two fingers I just pulled out of her pussy in her mouth, I slapped her ass cheeks as they waved back at me. Kapri had me wishing those two fingers was my dick; she bobbed her head up and down giving me what I wished was some sloppy top. Her tongue curled around my shit as she came up my middle finger slowly and grazed my fingertips; my nut started building up quick as I reminisced on her head game. Wrapping my free hand around her throat, I choked her gently, bending down to whisper in her ear.

"You miss sucking this dick, don't you?" I grunted with my balls slapping her pussy.

"Make it cum, baby," she coached. I reached around to play with her clit and realized her hand was already there, rubbing that mutha-fucka stiff as her shit got wetter and...

"DAMN KAPRI!" I came deeeep in her shit; my baby boy was gonna hate me when he came out because I could've sworn I poked the top of his head by accident.

"See what you do to me, Atif?" she whined with my hands grip-ping her waist. "You make me so fuckin' wet I just wanna climb on top of you and fuck you silly. Can I fuck you silly, baby?"

"Kapri my mama 'nem here," I laid on the bed and watched her climb on top. For her, he bricked back up immediately; he never got soft. "Come ride a big dick on a real G. Cum for your man and let that hurt go." I gripped him while she slid that sweet back and forth across the tip.

"You ain't even show me what that mouth do this morning," she gyrated her hips back and forth like she was riding a mechanical bull. She slid up and popped her hips back before dropping down on my meat; where the hell she got that shit from I have no idea.

"I'm sorry, baby." Kapri loved getting that pussy sucked, I was so focused on sliding in that I forgot. "I gotchu tonight."

"Just let me sit on your face real quick, I'm trying to see some-thing," she whispered in my ear. If I hadn't already nutted in her, I would've let her get hers too.

"What you trying to do, baby? You already pregnant.... FUCK GIRL!" she made me nut for the second time in five minutes with her signature move. Leaning down to suck my neck, I felt her teeth graze my skin as she squeezed every drop of cum out of me with her pussy muscles. That was the last thing I remembered; Kapri had me sleep and she was still on top. I ain't gonna be able to do shit, this woman gonna kill me with her love.

## TWENTY-FIVE
## KAPRI

I had to dig deep in my bag of tricks to put Atif back to bed, but that shit worked. He probably thought he was gonna have me down for the count, but I switched it up on his ass. Atif was going crazy with me not putting my mouth on him and I knew it; so, I did to his fingers what I would normally do to him. After he came the first time I knew it was a matter of minutes once I worked my hips and milked his ass dry. Baby was snoring before I got up to stretch.

After cleaning myself up for a second time, I called sis. "Tanji, you on your way up here?"

"Mmhmm. Mama said she haven't seen you since the boys left, she miss y'all."

"Oh, I'ma go see her this week. You know we gotta be in Wisconsin for that meetup by 8:30, where you at?"

"Bout to pull up now, see you in a few minutes."

"Bitch, I ain't got no clothes on," I giggled. "Go to the gas station or something, make it ten."

"Ten minutes? Atif must be over there giving you that Vitamin D!" she chuckled slightly.

"Nah, I was like Cardi B at Coachella on that ass, he ain't know what hit him," I cackled, trying to make her smile. "Atif in here snoring, girl."

"You stupid," she snickered in my ear. "Lemme go get some road snacks, I'll see you in ten minutes."

"Okay." Hanging up, I went to my closet to grab a cute t-shirt dress and some thigh high Fendi boots. That's all I wore; dresses and sandals or boots depending on my mood. Lately Atif was licking his lips every time he saw me. Fuck a Free, he knew who his real wife was. Sliding on a thong so he didn't get mad about me not wearing panties because I was pregnant, I slipped some gloss on my lips and pressed them together tightly. Snatching my shades from the dresser, I grabbed my Gucci clutch purse, gave Atif a peck on the lips before I left since he was still asleep, and bounced out the front door.

"Bitch you cute," Tanji complimented me once I got in the car. "Where you get that dress from?"

"PressedATL.com. Atif hates everything Fashion Nova sells," I giggled. "Said everybody wear that shit. Plus, I like how they clothes fit."

"I'ma have to check Mrs. Frost out then," she nodded approvingly. "On another note though, we need to run through today's play one more time."

"We sit down and talk to her about getting some work from her because we setting up shop in Rockford. I tried reaching out to God, but he not answering his phone," I began. "We were negotiating prices with Prince until he disappeared into thin air. We figured they didn't want no money, so we sent word out and got her information from some niggas in Maywood."

"And if she ask who?"

"We can't give her that info. That's street law; never give up your connect. You leave the streets starving if they get popped off, then niggas start plotting up on you."

"Why can't we just tell her Jeff gave us her information?"

"Jeff work for Free."

"He work for Free?" Tanji was quiet for a second, fidgeting with her purse strap as we rode up I-94. "Wait. Prince and Jeff talked all the time."

"Jeff set Prince up."

Tanji's eyes were cold as she processed my words. "Jeff set Prince up." It was more of a statement than a question. "How you find out?"

"Going through Atif's phone looking for Free's number." I felt it; the rush of bitterness and pain as it welled up in her spirit. Tanji was about to explode; I needed her to channel that energy into this meeting.

"So, because of this jealous hearted muthafucka, my baby girl won't grow up with her daddy," she shook, the vein in her neck twitching. "Because of this rat bastard, my daughter cries herself to sleep in my arms EVERY night. BECAUSE OF THIS BITCH ASS NIGGA, MY LOVE IS FUCKING GONE!" she slapped the window with each word she spoke.

Hearing that hurt in her voice, I changed my mind. Shit, I wasn't gonna try and talk her back from the edge. Tanji took Prince's death HARD. Not only was Jenesis sleeping with her every night, his urn laid on his pillow next to her as well. They stuck Steve out in Forest Home Cemetery and moved on with life; Tanji hadn't visited the man yet and he was her husband. "Sis we got bullets for both of these bitches, don't stress yourself out."

"Kapri, I'm pregnant," she whispered. "Prince gave me one last gift before he left."

"SIIIIIIS!" I screamed as we pulled up to the toll road. "I'm happy for you!"

"We gonna make it out of this, right Kapri?" she spoke quietly once we crossed the state line.

"Right."

"What if we don't?"

"Hell hath no fury like our men," I spoke with a straight face. "I know for a fact a couple of moves Prince put in place before he died, so we don't have to worry about Nuritsa popping up. Plus, Atif knows her whole family; her father will find himself dead in prison and not from natural causes either. That is, if he ain't already."

"Nuritsa, Nuritsa...that bitch from the hospital?"

"Mmhmm. Prince already had it set up for her to get popped off the next day," I schooled. "Just because he passed on don't mean the hustle stop, we get it how we live it."

"That's my Prince," she whispered to herself. "Gotta make sure the family straight above all."

"Now let's honor his memory by deading this bitch," I growled as we came off the expressway, putting our war faces on.

## TWENTY-SIX

## TANJI

Not for nothing, but Kapri was in the wrong profession. Life coach was definitely her calling, because I was messed up driving up to Kenilworth from downtown by myself. Once she got in the car, I felt a lot better, until she revealed that Jeff killed my Prince. So when we pulled up to the Cracker Barrel in Kenosha, I was ready to do more than that back and forth yatta-yatta; the gun in my clutch needed to be busting at somebody once it was all said and done. From what Kapri told me though, law enforcement in Wisconsin took their positions a lot more serious than the police in the Chi. I needed to calm down and let Kapri lure Free into one of these corn fields out here, then shoot that bitch.

After giving the hostess our names, she led us to the table where Free, Atif's wife, sat quietly in a corner of the restaurant by herself looking like a bag of nickels. Yea she had the labels, but her face was one that only a mother could love. He couldn't have possibly walked down that aisle sober.

"Hi! Free, right?" Kapri extended her hand out politely while I turned my head to keep from laughing in her face.

"Yes, yes, I am Free," she responded warmly. "Richie Rich, right?"

"That's us. I'm Richie, she's Rich. Short for Richelle," Kapri lied with ease. "Our mothers were best friends and thought it would be cute if they named us both the same thing, so here we are. It's just easier for us to refer to ourselves as one person instead of trying to explain the story to everyone we meet, since we make moves together."

"I see," she nodded. "You Americans have such strange customs. Have you ladies eaten breakfast yet?" she quickly changed the subject, smiling slightly while staring at Kapri's baby bump.

"I had a little something before I left home, and we been snacking this whole ride, so we're actually good," I spoke up. "Shall we get down to business?"

"Of course. My apologies, it's my understanding that my personal assistant set this up a while ago, and I'm only now hearing of it when you ladies reached out. Can you explain to me again what type of partnership you're looking to create?"

"Sure. Like I was telling Nuritsa..." Kapri began.

"Nuritsa is no longer my employee," Free interrupted curtly. Kapri kicked me under the table because I think she knew I was about to go in on this bad bodied, monkey faced hoe. "Start from the beginning."

"No problem." Kapri ran down the entire play word for word so smooth even I believed we had three trap houses and twenty niggas in Rockford ready to go.

"Why you come here? Why didn't you go to someone in Chicago?" she questioned slyly.

"We ain't from out here, we from Minnesota," I began. "I got people in Maywood, so when I asked, they gave us somebody name God information? You know him?"

Her whole facial expression changed, but we didn't let on that we noticed it. "I know Atif."

"Well, we reached out to this God person, but he never responded." Kapri continued. "Then we got somebody name Prince info and was talking to him for a minute, then he stopped answering his phone too."

"What's wrong wit' them niggas? They don't like money?" I asked, twirling the ring on my finger that I found in Prince's things.

"You came to the right place," Free poured sugar in the steaming cup of black coffee that the waitress placed in front of her. "How much do you ladies need?"

"Starting out, we trying to get five a piece," Kapri expressed. "We see how that goes, if it's good we'll be in touch."

"Five is good," Free smiled. "Do you have cash?"

"Of course we have cash, muthafuckas out here trying to PayPal some dope?" I snickered. "Where you wanna meet up?"

"Not here. I have a house down the street where we can do business. That way you can meet my associate and work with him from this point on."

I pinched Kapri under the table, was this bitch trying to set us up? She responded with a gentle tap to my thigh and I was okay. "That's doable. Gimme the address and we can work that out," she spoke confidently.

After exchanging information, we made small talk about the weather and Kapri's due date before we headed out. "You trust this trick?"

"Doesn't matter whether I trust her or not, according to Google Maps this 'house down the street' of hers is in the middle of nowhere," Kapri replied with a straight face, adjusting her Cartier frames. "Perfect spot as far as I'm concerned."

"What about this associate of hers? Kapri, I don't like this one bit," I rubbed the spot where my embryo should be, since I wasn't showing yet.

Kapri stopped the car in the middle of turning out the parking lot, blocking traffic in the process.

"You know what, Tanji? You can go. I'll even drop you off at that hotel we passed and come back to pick you up. I'm riding for my brother though," she spat as the people in the cars behind us leaned on their horns.

"She stole my baby from my baby," I turned and stared out the window when Prince's voice whispered in my ear that he loved me. "I'm in."

"Good, 'cause I was gonna talk about yo' ass all the way back to the city," she giggled.

# TWENTY-SEVEN

# ATIF

"You said she where?"

"Fuck she doing in Wisconsin?"

"How the hell YOU know and I don't?"

"Look, AZ, make sure nothing happens to wifey, man."

"Good look, G." I ended the call.

AZ was blowing my phone up back to back; then when I answered that's what he had to tell me. No wonder she was creeping in and out of this house at all hours of the day; Kapri called herself going after Free and took Tanji's ass with her. Why she thought that made sense and she was pregnant with my first child was beyond me.

Scrolling to her number in my phone, I called her just to see if she'd pick up and just as I suspected, she didn't. I sent her a text, then walked inside our closet to find my black V-neck Hanes tee and a pair of black jeans. Stepping inside my secret closet, I went looking for my favorite pistol and saw it was gone. So was my second favorite gun. "This girl gonna be the death of me. Most likely she gonna be the death of Free, but after that," I shook my head, grabbing the .357 before tucking in in my waist.

"Atif I'm frying the kids some chicken and smothered potatoes with green peas and rolls, your father wants seafood gumbo, and I'm trying to see what Kapri..." My mother stopped when she walked in my closet, seeing me down on one knee with the trap compartment in the floor wide open. "Why are you in there?"

"Mama..."

"Atif, you promised me that you'd never go in that hatch. Why is it opened?"

"Kapri in Wisconsin."

Mama covered her mouth with trembling hands; I watched her eyes become heavy as she stood frozen in place. "Do what you gotta do, son. Bring my baby girl home."

Staring at the guns remaining, I closed my eyes and said a brief prayer for Allah to cover my wife and son until I got there.

"I will Mama."

No words were said after that; I grabbed the keys to my trap truck and left her standing there. My body was telling me 'not yet', but my heart asked why I was still in Illinois. I had to get to her.

---

I FOUND out why my Bluetooth would pop on whenever I got a phone call, it was set to auto answer. I don't be fucking with these cars and shit, long as it start up when I turn the key or put gas in it, I'm good. So when Kapri's phone called me back in the middle of me beating Rick Ross' part on that Hard Piano on Pusha T's Daytona album, I was set to cuss her out for putting herself in a dangerous position in the first place.

"Kapri what the fuck...Hello? KAPRI!"

She wasn't answering me. I was beginning to think her phone called me on its own so I would know what she was up to. Turning the volume on the call up, I focused on her voice over all the screaming and yelling in the background.

SMACK! Something hard thumped against what I assume was the floor. *Was that my wife?* "Free's right hand?" Tanji's voice cackled as I heard the clicking noises of my favorite pistol. "Tuh! Nigga look soft like baby shit to me!"

Someone hocked spit out of their throat, splatting thickly against a hard surface. "You know what made my day? Seeing that nigga beating against the windows as he burned to death...AAAHHH!" a male voice taunted.

"Wanna know what's about to make my day, BITCH!" Tanji screamed as the hammer pulled back on that pistol followed quickly by a loud boom. Two other booms followed behind the first as Kapri laughed crazily.

"GET THAT MUTHAFUCKA SIS! REVENGE YO' MUTHAFUCKIN' MAN!" she screamed. *First, she singing Tupac in the shower, now she out here coaching plays? Who the fuck did I get pregnant?*

A door opened and slammed, heels clacked inside of the space where they were as I mashed the gas pedal to the floor, running the speedometer up to 100 mph. "What is going on here?" Free's voice questioned angrily. "Who are you?"

"This the bitch ya husband in love with!" Tanji screamed. "Got you worried about whether or not your stepchild ate, that's so sweet."

"Ahh, Kapri," Free uttered gutturally. "I'm only going to say this to you one time and one time only. Give me Atif and we can settle this war. If not, I shoot both of you, then go blow up your home in Kenilworth. What do you say?"

"Feeelllings....bitch you all in your feeelllings...even though you don't liiikkkee meeee...hoe you ain't gonna fight meeee..." Kapri sang. That was my jam; knowing them they was probably over there dancing too.

"Oooohhh...and I bet cha don't want it with meee cause thot you too thirstyyy singin' wad up, fuck up. Ba-dee-daaahhh-dah, get fucked up," Tanji finished. "Bitch look at you and look at my sissy. This Atif's lil' chocolate drop, sweet like Kool-Aid. Then look at you, standing over there shaped like grandma's knee cap. Blowing shit up like that's gonna make him love you," she giggled. They don't need to be together no more after this.

Hearing that familiar click a second time, I tried pulling her up on Find My iPhone; AZ said the address she sent him was in the middle of nowhere, and since Free...BOOM! BOOM! BOOM! BOOM!

Staring at the Bluetooth screen as I crossed the state line, I realized the phone hung up on its own. "SHIT!"

# TWENTY-EIGHT
## KAPRI

"I just wanna know HOW YOU MISSED!" Tanji yelled, stomping her foot while pointing at the door. Free's peacock blue Louboutin heels were still sitting at the front door where she herself stood only moments ago.

"Blame Atif's son, this boy kicked me in my bladder when I aimed at his step-mee-mee," I cackled, rubbing my round stomach. "That bitch can run though, can't she?"

"Hell yeah," Tanji laughed with me, peeking through the blinds looking for her. "Her car gone already too."

"Saw that pistol come out and had keys in hand! She was NOT PLAYING with these folks!" I died laughing at Atif's wife.

We came down here and Jeff was posted up in the house. Free did a quick introduction and left us alone with this muthafucka. I don't know if the plan was to rob us because we was green or what, but that shit was thwarted quickly. Soon as she got down the road, Tanji busted him across the head with her pistol and we had that ass tied up in a corner by the time he came to. Tanji asked him a simple question, why he killed her husband? She'd already found the wedding band and seven carat round diamond in his luggage that he packed for our trip to Miami before the accident.

Instead of him just answering the question as asked, he decided that he wanted to talk shit, taunting that girl about how Prince died. First shot was dead between his eyes; Tanji was a quick learner when it came to weapons. Second shot was to the heart, and the third was to the balls. As she was in the midst of spitting on his corpse, the door opened and in walked Free looking just a little perturbed. While Tanji was destroying the woman's hopes and dreams of remaining Siranush Hermes, I was pulling the pistol out of my clutch. Raising my hand, I aimed at her head when Atif Jr., kicked me hard in my pelvis. This baby play too much. Anyway, I blinked and by the time I opened my eyes she'd ran out of her shoes leaving the front door to the abandoned house on Washington Road wide open.

Checking the house and Jeff's car, we discovered my assumption was correct: Jeff didn't have no dope, but he did have a few guns, a box of hollow point bullets, and some rope. Free just saved her own life and didn't even know it. Leaving the door wide open, we walked back to our car and got ready to go. "Since we missed this time, we might as well...wait, who is that?" Tanji questioned, pointing at a truck speeding towards us. I pulled my gun out and held it tightly to my side and slightly behind my back as it approached.

"No this bitch didn't call herself...hol' up...I know that truck," I squinted. "Fuckin' AZ! Can't tell that muthafucka NOTHING!"

"Kapri, who is that?"

I pulled out my phone and sent him a text, telling him he should be disbarred for snitching on me. "Atif." My text ringer dinged; AZ replied with all laughing emojis.

"KAPRI!" he yelled my name out the window, driving slightly past where we stood before throwing his vehicle in park aggressively. "Fuck is you doing up here playing American Gangster with my baby?" he climbed out the truck, slamming the door so hard I thought he broke the glass.

"I ain't playing nothing baby, what you talking about?" I beamed, sliding up close to him to rub his chest. "Me and Tanji thinking about buying this house and flipping it."

"Oh, for real?" he pulled out his phone, flashing his call log at me. "What was you doin' bout twenty minutes ago then?"

I glanced at the log, which clearly had my name on the screen for a ten minute call. I didn't call Atif; he didn't need to know what I was up to in Wisconsin. Ol' broke ass iPhone 8; I was taking this shit back to Apple soon as I got to the city. "Baby let me..."

"GET YO' ASS IN THE TRUCK, GIRL!" he grabbed my arm and pushed me towards his vehicle. "And Tanji you get yo' ass in that car and I'm following you back to the city! I should be whupping both of y'all asses right now!"

"Atif you can't tell me to..." Tanji began, but when she saw the look of murder in his eyes, she shut her ass up and got in that car.

"Just because we expecting a baby together and we something like engaged don't make you my daddy, you know," I sulked, folding my arms over my chest and poking my bottom lip out. He leaned over and grabbed my lip between his teeth gently while running his hand up my inner thigh.

"Pussy still hot, huh," he moaned. "That street shit got yo' ass percolating, you ready to fuck ain't you?"

"Mmhmm," my eyes rolled in the back of my head. "That shit feel good."

"I am yo' muthafuckin' daddy," he mumbled, tickling my earlobe with his tongue as he slid two fingers in my pussy. "Daddy tell you to stay home while you pregnant with my baby, that's what the fuck you do, you hear me?"

"Fuck...Atif..."

"Matter of fact, you drive. I'ma show yo' hardheaded ass that when I tell you to do something, you fuckin' do it." We switched seats as Tanji waited patiently for us to pull off. Soon as I got in the driver's seat and turned on the ignition, Atif spread my legs before snatching my thong off and buried his face between my thighs. His lips felt good sucking the inside of each thigh, grazing his teeth gently across my skin before touching the sore spot with the tip of his tongue.

"Atiiiif....wait...wait..."

"Drive Kapri," he mumbled, not letting up his alternating assault on me. I tried pulling onto the road, but when he slid his tongue rapidly up and down my slit, I damn near hit a tree when that orgasm slammed against his face.

"FUUUUCK BABY!" he wasn't stopping no time soon; my legs were shaking, and he was still tongue kissing my sex. "I PROMISE! ATIF I PROMISE!"

"Promise what?" he stopped briefly to ask before continuing his linguistic abuse. I swear I love this man.

"I'LL...FUUUCK!"

"You already fucking, baby," he moaned. "What you promise?"

"I'll...ATIF PLEASE!"

"You want me to keep going?"

"NO! Oh God, no!"

"Since you remembered who I am, I'll forgive you." He stopped playing and sat up. Sliding his fingers back inside me while slipping his tongue in my mouth, his wet beard rubbed against my face, tickling my chin.

"Say three 'Hail Kapris', and you're forgiven." I smiled before he said it. "You can drive now baby, I'm going to sleep."

"Your stubborn ass should've been sleep, all in Wisconsin shootin' at folks," he chuckled as I climbed in the back seat.

"Had you taken care of it in the first place, I wouldn't have to be here," I grumbled sleepily, tucking into the seat.

"Don't worry baby. You won't be back up here after today," I heard him speak lowly as my eyelids fluttered closed.

# TWENTY-NINE

# TANJI

Riding back to the city followed by Kapri and the God, I felt Prince's spirit in the car with me. If he was alive, I would've gotten that same cuss out that Kapri got. On the other hand, my love could rest well in heaven knowing that the bastard who initiated his death was in an abandoned house in Wisconsin that nobody owned. By the time they found his body, he would be unrecognizable; I saw the rats huddled in the corner making plans before we left.

Turning the radio to Power 92.3, I started snapping my fingers when that one song came on that I forgot the name of, but I loved the beat. My phone rang as soon as the song went off and the commercial came on. I thought I put Monica on do not disturb after that whole *'no baby'* incident, being as how she was currently ringing my phone, I must've forgot.

"Yeah."

"Hello, Tanjalyn? This is Tangelica Morse. I'm calling because you and I have some things to discuss."

Not only did she not let me get a word in, but she actually had the audacity to be calling me on Monica's line. I knew that bitch was stupid. "Such as?"

"First and foremost, I think you and I should be able to get along like two grown women instead of bickering back and forth like we're uncivilized," she began. "Second..."

"Lemme interrupt you right there, Tangelica. I am civilized, you see I haven't set foot in Steve's mother's home since the day I picked up my children and you were there. A lesser woman would've beat yo' muthafuckin' ass by now."

"There's no need for swearing," she chastised. "Lesser women who aren't educated are the ones who use curse words."

"Good fucking thing I hold a Master's Degree in Public Administration with a specialization in International Public Management, ain't it bitch?" I chuckled. "Steve never did find out about me taking them online classes at DePaul. By the way, what school you graduate from, hoe?"

"That's not important," she stuttered. "What is important is..."

"Mmhmm." I rolled my eyes, hard. "Cut the shit, what you want, Tangelica?"

"I just think we should put our personal dislike for each other to the side for the sake of our children. We can be civil towards one another so they can bond, right?"

"If them kids was Steve's, sure. But since they ain't —"

"Oohoo, I have a DNA test that says they are!"

Who raised this woman? She interrupted every sentence out of my mouth.

"Well, did you give that to the military? This can be cleared up easy, right?"

"See, this is just between us, why do we need the government all in our business?" she spoke kindly. Tangelica sounded like a baby daddy begging to be took off of child support. "They can't control anything we set up between us."

"Have a nice life, Hoe-nasia," I matched her tone and was about to hang up when I heard her yelling in the phone.

"Tanji, Steve gave me a copy of Jenesis' DNA test. You can go to jail for lying to the military!"

"Says the thot who got a fake DNA!" I yelled back. "Legally he is her father; he signed her birth certificate. You can't come no better than that?"

"Oh, just so you know, I saw when that sexy light skin poured gasoline all over y'all house on Drexel after he beat up the love of my life," she growled. "I'm sure the police wouldn't mind seeing it too."

I turned the radio down to make sure I heard her correctly. "What you say?"

"You know damn well what I said. Them two sexy light skins that broke in your house that night? Jenesis kissed one of them on the cheek while the other one pretended like he was about to kidnap you? I'm sure the judge would love to know how hard it was watching as the one with the tattoos on his neck beat the life out of poor old Steve," she spat evilly.

"We should meet up." I pulled over on the side of the expressway with Kapri right behind me. "What hotel are you staying at?"

"The Four Seasons downtown, of course," she spoke haughtily. "Seven o'clock sharp," she stressed before hanging up.

God came up on the right side of my car beating on the window. "Damn, you gonna crack my glass!"

"Fuck this glass. What's wrong wit'chu?"

"Uhmm...nothing."  .

"Nothing, huh. Tanji don't let me find out something wrong and I find out too fuckin' late!"

"Steve's bitch say she got a copy of the video from when you and Prince killed Steve."

"Ain't this some shit," he replied a little too calm. "What she plan on doing with this video?"

"Going to the police. What's wrong with you and Prince? Y'all don't react to nothing!"

"Cause this small shit to a giant." He tapped the top of my car before walking back to his. "Go home an' put ya feet up, sis. Big bro got'chu."

I rolled the window down and stuck my head out, yelling over the cars as they whizzed by on the expressway. "Atif, what about..."

"Tanji, do what I said for once, damn! Stop stressing over this street shit!"

*I'ma keep fucking with Atif and he gonna kick my ass,* I snickered to myself, rolling the window back up.

They say if you give a bitch a bone, she'll take it out in the world and bring you back two. That's exactly what Monica came over my house sniffing around for, a small lil' chicken bone that she could turn into a T-bone before she took it back to her mother and her 'real' sister-in-law about me and Prince. That's why I kept it cordial and let her do all the talking. Now that Tangelica knew that I knew about this video, she wanted to talk. Tuh. AZ was gonna eat that shit up so fast in court that Tangelica Morse would look up and find herself sitting in somebody's projects wondering why the roaches scattered every time she turned on the light. Judging from the look on God's face a second ago, that video wasn't gonna see daylight. Monica act like she know so much about God and Prince, she should've told her they was some savages.

# THIRTY

## ATIF

I had to look out for Tanji now with the Prince gone. I knew if the shoe was on the other foot, he'd do the same for me. I also made sure his mama was good; even though I hadn't been over there yet, I talked to her every day. Ma Dukes stopped over her spot too since she was here; they were good friends before she moved. Prince had to be looking down on the real G's with a smile.

The fact that Kapri felt the need to go up to Wisconsin to get at my wife had me tight, but I understood her motives. Man...that ride back to the city was quiet than a muthafucka; on one hand I wanted to cuss her out, on the other I wanted to lean the seat back and give her some 'it's-the-thought-that-counts' dick. I didn't need my woman to fight my battles for me; I was who I was because I know how to hold my own plus more. Hence the reason I checked to make sure my wife was sleep before I called the chick who, according to the court system, was my wife too.

"Atif. I knew you'd call," Free breathed in my ear. "Are you coming home?"

"What was your point behind sending two women, one of whom is visibly pregnant, to an abandoned house with Jeff weak ass?"

She giggled coldly in my ear as I focused on the road. "Weak, huh. How 'weak' was he when he killed YOUR right hand?"

"That he ambushed like the hoe he is. Like I said, Jeff weak ass. A real nigga would've shot him in the head at point blank range, considering how many opportunities he had before that." I buffed my nails on my shirt imagining the look on her face. "If that's ya right hand, I see how he got killed by a chick who ain't even in the fucking game."

"If we combined our resources, we would be unstoppable," Free ignored me to talk about this female Armenian mob. "Bigger than the Gotti family. The modern day Capones of Chicago. Since the streets know you as God, I can be...I can be..."

"You can be another dumb bitch trying to fuck the God," I spat in her ear. "You met my wife. Sexy, ain't she?"

"Now that I know what she looks like, I'm going to kill your 'wife', Atif. Hope you got a good deal on Prince's cremation because you're going to need it. Maybe they'll give you a two for one special; I got a bullet with her little friend's name on it too. Love you, babe," she cackled before she hung up.

"Your wife is hilarious," Kapri spoke from behind me. "Two can play that game."

"Two can, but two ain't," I spoke gruffly so she understood where I was coming from. "Yo ass bout to go to Atlanta. And before you open your mouth, ya girl going too. I ain't taking no chances with you, my baby, or lil' sis."

"Atlanta? Atif..."

"Kapri, this ain't up for discussion. I'm calling Pop now, so he can get the jet gassed up and call the pilot. Go chill at Ma Dukes crib; she got a condo in Midtown overlooking the city. It's nice as fuck."

"What about you? Atif I can't lose you twice," she protested, leaning forward to kiss the back of my neck while reaching around to run her fingers through my beard.

"You not gonna lose me, Kapri. I promise."

"How do I know that, though?" she whimpered. I felt a hot tear splash against my skin as she laid her head on my shoulder.

"Trust ya man. Have I broken a promise to you yet?"

"No."

"This situation won't be the one that I start, then."

"I don't wanna go to Atlanta. I wanna go home with you," she cried softly.

"Daddy will be home, baby don't cry," I turned my head slightly and kissed the tip of her nose. "Ma gonna take good care of you and the boys, okay?"

"Okay," she sniffed. "Come get me when this is over, okay?"

"I will, love. I will."

---

TELLING POP that Ma had to go back to Atlanta until this whole thing blew over had him on go. I didn't get my doggish ways from him; my mother could snap her fingers and no matter where he was in the world he dropped everything for her. Nah, I got my savageness from the streets. Ever since I met Kapri though, I was beginning to understand Pop's reasoning more and more.

We detoured to the airport and were waiting for Prince's mother and kids to pull up. Like I said before, I wasn't taking any chances with any of the women in my life. The source of a woman's scorn is always another woman, and as far as I was concerned Free could be coming for either of these four. What she didn't know was Prince's father was also a made man in Armenia; once he found out about his son, she was on his shit list too.

"Atif, is there a Six Flags Great America in Atlanta?" Jacoby asked excitedly. "I wanna go ride the rides!"

"There's a Six Flags, but it's not called Great America, it's Six Flags over Georgia." I rubbed my hand over his waves. The older he got, the more that boy looked like his biological mother, who was standing off to the side away from everyone else rubbing her baby bump worriedly.

"Can we go, Atif? Please?"

"We'll go when I come down, okay?"

"Kapri can't take us?" Jacari frowned, staring at me with his eyebrow raised. He was the one who was gonna give me the most trouble when he got older.

"Yo sister pregnant. She can take you, but she can't get on no rides. That ain't right, is it?"

"I guess you good for now." He shrugged his shoulders in my direction before going to stand near his sister. Yeah, we was gonna have a little power struggle once he got a few strings of facial hair in a few years. I turned and noticed my mother chuckling at us as Prince's mother shook her head.

"What?"

"Nothing," they both spoke at the same time before turning to walk away, nudging each other and pointing back at me as they got on the plane.

Before she got on the aircraft good, Pop grabbed Ma by the waist and pulled her close as Prince's mother smiled at them both. He whispered in her ear and she stood giggling at whatever private moment they were in the midst of. A tap on the shoulder had me turning around grabbing my pistol at first, but when I saw who it was I gave him some dap.

"Whaddup, Unc. Man, I ain't seen you in years!"

"I know, I know. It's good to see you again, Atif," he replied warmly. Prince's father Vahan was a little flashier than my own; he always had been. Me and Zadrian were the exact opposite of our fathers; seeing them and us together you'd think we were switched at birth. As usual, Vahan was standing in front of me dressed in black silk Versace pajamas with a matching smoking jacket and slippers fresh off the plane. Reaching up to adjust his Balenciaga frames, I noticed his jet black hair was beginning to show silver streaks. Of course he was wearing an exclusive diamond encrusted Audemars that was, no doubt, designed exclusively for him underneath his thick gold bracelet twinkling in the afternoon sun. I loved this man's swag; he knew all the top designers personally. Donatella had him on speed dial, and he had lunch with Serge, Ferruccio, and Giorgio, fashion's top O.G.'s in the game, every week.

"I see Aram and Philomené," he pointed out, puffing on his cigar. "Where's..."

"Vahan." Prince's mother stood at the entrance of Pop's private jet. I left them all to catch up, I had to have a pep talk with my boys.

"Jacari! Jacoby! Aye, lemme holla at y'all real quick." They both came to where I stood at the bottom of the steps. "Listen, I'm putting the most important people to me on this jet. That includes both of y'all. I'm talking to y'all as men in case I don't come back."

"Why wouldn't you come back, Atif?" Jacoby asked inquisitively.

"That's what happens sometimes out here, 'Coby," Jacari schooled his little brother. "Every now and then gangstas gotta take that L."

"I'm not a gangsta," I corrected him. "I'm the GOD. There's a difference. Gangstas report to anotha muthafucka for guidance. I'm the otha muthafucka they report to. This goes beyond boss status, I am their first and their last. Understand?"

"Damn, God, you got it like that?" Jacari slipped up.

"I'ma let you slide, but don't be cussing around these women," I chastised him a little. He was growing into a man; I didn't want to tell him not to cuss, but I didn't want him to think he could say what he wanted whenever he wanted. "Take care of your sister. Make sure she's happy. If she ain't, find out why she ain't happy and get it for her. If I don't come back, she won't be happy for a while, y'all be there to help her get through it, a'ight?"

"Okay. Who is that man?" Jacoby asked, pointing at Prince's father who was whispering in his girl's ear with his arms around her waist while she blushed. Man, lil' bro would've loved to see this; his parents all boo'ed up like they used to be back in the day.

"Prince's father and your great uncle. That's what we call an O.G."

"Is Grandad an O.G. too?" Jacari questioned with a small smile threatening to take over his face.

"Those two men over there are the ultimate O.G.'s. That's who I wanted to be like when I was y'all age, but not what I want for y'all. I want y'all to go to school, get y'all a couple of degrees, and make me and ya sister proud. Be our success stories. Can y'all do that for me?"

"We got'chu, 'Tif," both boys nodded their heads and gave me dap.

"A'ight, look like the pilot trying to take off. Have fun in the A and I'll see y'all in a few days. If I don't see y'all, don't forget what we talked about, a'ight?" I nudged both of them towards the aircraft sitting patiently on the tarmac.

"Aye 'Tif," Jacari stopped first and Jacoby followed.

"Whaddup lil' bro?"

"Aye, I know real G's don't say this, but we love you." Both boys threw their arms around me and hugged me tightly. I wrapped my arms around them both, pecking them on the top of their waves.

"Real G's might not say it, but real men do. I love y'all too, a'ight?"

"A'ight," their watery voices spoke.

"Come on now, wipe ya eyes and poke ya lil chests out. Be strong for these women, a'ight?"

"Okay." Jacoby was still sniffing and wiping his eyes; Jacari did a quick swipe and he was good.

After helping them up the steps, I turned to their big sister. "Come here, Pooh."

Walking slowly to where I stood, she burst into tears, resting her head on my shoulder. "Don't forget your promise to me," she wept softly.

"That would mean I'd have to forget you and we can't have that, can we?" I murmured in her ear, kissing her earlobe. "I need you to be strong for my baby boy." Getting down on one knee in front of her, I rubbed her belly for good luck, touching my head to her belly button. "Be strong for Daddy, son. Keep your mama calm so you can come into this world surrounded by love and light." For the first time, he reached out and I felt what was either his hand or his foot rub against my forehead.

"We love you, baby." She reached down and touched my cheek as my son reassured me of her words.

"I love you too." I stood up and wrapped my tongue around hers one last time before she got on that jet and left me. "See you in a few days."

"Okay," she whispered, wrapping her arms around my neck. I squeezed her once more, not wanting to let go.

"Atif! Come on, we got women we tryin' to get back to too!" Pop yelled from my trap truck.

"Pop gonna whup yo ass, you better go," she chided, kissing my cheek as I smacked her ass.

"Pop gonna whup YO ass, you know how he is about Ma Dukes. I'll call you tonight and let you know what happened, a'ight?"

"Okay, love."

# THIRTY-ONE

# KAPRI

"Mama, it's gonna be okay, right? He's gonna be okay, right?" I watched him walk to his truck with that cocky, confident swagger that made me fall in love with him that night at Burger King. If I lived forever, I'll never forget the sexiest thing he's ever said to me: *Bad lil' thang, fine as hell. Like I said before, you mine. So, if you got a nigga, let him know the God is coming for him. And if you don't got a nigga, let these muthafuckas know you belong to the God. See you around, shaw—Kapi. Short for Kapri.*

"Atif's gonna be fine, my love," she reassured me, stroking my hair. "Trust me when I tell you that those two men he's with would rather give up their own lives before they allow something to happen to him. I'm the one who should be worried!"

"Me too, sweetie," Virginie came over and sat with us. "First, I lose my only son, and to lose his father on top of that would break me. I don't know how I'd come back from that."

"I thought you hadn't seen him in years though?" I was confused.

"Girl," she giggled, patting me on my knee. "I live in one of Chicago's roughest neighborhoods, but have you ever seen or heard any gunshots on my block? Niggas selling dope all hours of the night?"

"No."

"Seen any graffiti on the side of the buildings? Trash on the street?"

"No."

"Does anyone ride down my block beating loud music? Stray dogs or cats out?"

Now that I thought about it, I didn't. "That's all Vahan?"

"I own the block. Every building on it is mine. Them folks ain't my neighbors, they my tenants. Any loud noise, arguing, anything that disrupts my peace and I evict that ass. Vahan didn't leave me out here struggling, between him, my son, and my nephew, I don't want for anything!" she smiled.

"Get that money, auntie!" I high fived her. "If you hadn't said nothing I would've thought you just stayed on the nice side of the block. Don't pay me no attention, I'd rather have Atif than anything he's ever given me."

"I know. I'd rather have Vahan, but I don't want to live out there and he don't want to move back here. We both stubborn as hell, guess who inherited those traits, Tanji?" she giggled, pulling her daughter-in-law into our conversation.

"Oooo, Jenesis is JUST like y'all!" she chuckled sadly. "Whenever y'all want her, PLEASE come get y'all baby!"

"Philomené, did I tell you about when my baby girl told me to call Atif and make him bring her daddy back?" she chuckled, rubbing Tanji's back. "Said her mommy didn't understand how much a princess needs her daddy and I did."

"I need her daddy too," Tanji whispered quietly as the tears began to roll. "Mama, what am I gonna do without him?"

"Same as you been doing, baby. You live. Be strong for his children, be strong for him. He knows you miss him, we all do. Keep him alive in your babies' hearts and their memories."

"I definitely will." She leaned her head on Virginie's shoulder while rubbing her little stomach.

"My son told me the day he passed that you were pregnant," Virginie revealed to Tanji's shock.

"He knew? How did he know? I didn't find out until after the funeral!"

"After he dropped Kapri off, he came and told me he felt like you might be pregnant again. You know these men know our bodies better than we do." Prince's mother snickered.

"Those is facts, Auntie V," I rubbed my baby bump, smiling as I thought back to when Atif told me we were having a boy. "And they stick together too," I spoke, glancing over at my brothers.

"Oh, they loyal to a fault!" Mama chuckled. "Vahan and Aram still thick as thieves! But that's what they taught their boys, who teaching it to their boys," she smiled, watching Jacari pull Steve Jr over to where they were playing the PlayStation.

"We are Armenian royalty, honey," Virginie patted my hand with a smile. "Our men are kings in their home country. This bitch Free don't know who she fucking with for real, she just think she know."

"Oh, but she about to find out though," Mama swiped through her phone until she found a video. "Look what your boo Vahan had done to that prison her father in."

Passing us her phone, we sat close together to watch as shadowy figures dropped dark packages in the night around a stone building. As we watched the time elapse on the feed sped up to 12 times the normal view. The video slowed down as the first cloud of smoke erupted from one side of the building. I saw a man being dangled from the roof by his ankles before being tossed over the side. A few minutes later, a helicopter hovered over the roof while the perpetrator climbed on the rope ladder. Once the helicopter left, you could see as the rest of the building detonated and collapsed all at once.

"Y'all know my man don't play!" Virginie hopped up and slapped five with Philomené. They cracked me up; both of them knew they was too old. Got grandkids and shit acting ratchet as ever.

"Girl, Aram had to tell them don't forget the man on the roof; you know Vahan was gonna leave him up there!" she cackled. "She-She made the bombs, though."

"She-She? Girl I ain't seen that heifer in years, I thought she was dead," they gossiped.

"Mmhmm. Now you know she ain't right. How you gonna make the bombs that you know they bout to kill your man with? She-She still ain't shit!" Philomené snickered.

"Wait, wait, waaaaait a minute," I stopped them both as Tanji looked on, both of us confused. "Who is She-She?"

"Siranush's mammy," Virginie rolled her eyes and popped her lips. "Philomené, remember when I had to punch her ass in the mouth over Vahan?"

"Free's mother?" Tanji questioned.

"That's what a mammy is," Virginie laughed.

"I remember when you punched her, that big bitch stood there dazed, then she tipped over and thudded on the ground!" Philomené cackled. "Nasty ass. Told Aram she didn't give a fuck what he did to that girl after he gave her that money to pay them folks."

"Did with who? Pay what folks? MAMA!"

"Oh, Kapri, I'm sorry baby. Your father-in-law gave Free's mother money to pay the judge off so he could overturn her husband's conviction and Atif wouldn't have to marry Siranush. Instead, she kept the money and threatened to blackmail Aram if Atif didn't marry her daughter. She was gonna tell everyone Aram raped Free the night before she married his son. What really happened was Aram went over there with two of his bodyguards and Free came on to them. It was consensual, but the story she seems to remember is that it wasn't. That's the lie her mother drilled in her head so much she believes it."

"How you know it wasn't?"

"First off, I believe my husband. He has no reason to lie to me about that bitch. Second, She-She don't give a fuck about nothing or nobody. She the best bomb maker in her country though; for the right price, she'll pin her own mama to the ceiling!" she laughed loudly.

"Lemme get this straight, this whole thing is over a lie that this She-She person told back in the day?"

"Actually, it's over a couple of thousand dollars," Virginie piped in. "The US dollar is worth a lot more in Armenia."

"Why didn't somebody just get the man out of jail and..."

"For one, She-She was so busy trying to give my man them nasty panties that she didn't want her husband out. For two, she had to marry that scarecrow off to somebody, why not a Hermes man? For three, some bitches just like to feel important. In this case, that bitch was She-She," Virginie finished.

"All y'all a hot ass mess," Tanji shrugged, grabbing some fruit from the cart in the cabin. "This better than any reality show on TV!"

"Either way, she bout to get what's coming to her," Virginie resolved. "Not only did this bitch kill my baby, but you don't threaten men like Aram and Vahan, so..."

"Girl, I miss you." Philomené laughed at her friend. "You think Vahan will let you move down to Atlanta?"

"LET me move? I ain't gotta ask him if I can go, I'll just get up and leave if that's what I wanna do!" Virginie protested with her eyebrow raised.

"Mmhmm. So you gonna ask him before he leave?"

"Yeah, I'ma see what he say," she snickered. "I think I want a house down there though. Maybe somewhere out in the country, he can have me one built while I stay...where you stay again?"

"Midtown. You know Aram built me a house way out in the country too."

"Girl, where? I might need your real estate agent's phone number."

I let them finish catching up and gossiping, nudging Tanji before pointing at them as they giggled and talked loudly. "You know that's gonna be us in about twenty years."

"Why was I just thinking the same thing?" she whispered back.

# THIRTY-TWO

# ATIF

"Pop, you must be going soft. Any bitch that threatens my family doesn't deserve mercy from me, ESPECIALLY not a bitch that threatens my pregnant wife!" I yelled in my father's direction.

"Atif, I never used the word mercy. What I said was that you should take her feelings into consideration, the woman is in love with you," Pop clarified.

Sitting across from him at the cigar bar downtown where we took over the back room for our meeting, I stared heatedly at the man who taught me to never show mercy on your enemies no matter who they were, telling me to show mercy towards this bitch. "I never agreed to marry the hoe. I did this for you. So if anyone should show her mercy, it should be you."

"Aram, why are we showing mercy to an enemy of the family? This woman instigated my son's murder. You saw the autopsy pictures; I plan to return the favor," Vahan growled viciously, chewing on the tip of his cigar.

"Rohan saved my life, this is about more than just his daughter. If it wasn't for him..."

"ROHAN IS DEAD! Any allegiance you think you may have

had to him died when we tossed his ass off of that roof! FUCK HIM! My son is dead, Aram! DEAD!" Vahan slammed his fist against the table. "An eye for a fucking eye!"

"Pop, sit this one out, bro. We should've sent you to the A with the women. Unc, I'm 'bout to get this bitch to the city." I whipped out my phone and shot her a text. "Stop trying to save these hoes, Pop."

"She seemed like such a sweet girl that night." Pop lit a second cigar and puffed lightly. "I couldn't believe it when she began taking her clothes off and doing what she did. Then for She-She to come and tell me she was going to the authorities for raping her daughter—"

"Look Aram. It's not your fault them bitches fucked up like that. She-She called me after the wedding talking 'bout that mob shit was a go and she didn't need me to help her get it started," Vahan puffed on his cigar while checking his text messages.

"Hold on, how long they been planning this mob shit?" I questioned with my hand up.

"Years," Pop revealed. "Rohan approached me about that shit when he first got popped off. I told him naw, it would take too much training, introductions, all that. Plus we don't deal with people we don't trust implicitly, especially with the amount of connections we have."

"An Armenian mob made up of all women? In Chicago? That would've been even worse than all men! Women too fucking emotional; they'd be trying to make deals, have these niggas out here singing kum-ba-yah, talking out their problems and cleaning up their own murders because they the ones that messed it up," he grumbled, sipping his cognac. "Even after you agreed to it, why would they think that I would?"

"I'ma say it for the millionth time: I DID NOT AGREE TO THAT!" Pop slapped the table to emphasize his words. "Eisha told She-She I was on board with that nonsense, I ain't said shit!"

"They'd still have to get their weapons from me," Unc continued. "She-She tried to pin a baby on me that she knew wasn't mine and damn near had Virginie kill me in my sleep. I wouldn't....ugh!" Vahan shivered with disgust. "That bitch stank."

"You used to fuck with Free's ol' girl, Unc?"

"Free's ol' girl tried giving me some pussy," he shook his head no, "but I gave that shit right back. Don't get me wrong, it wasn't her looks. It was never her looks. My woman ain't gotta be the baddest thing out here; as long as she got confidence and keep herself up, I can look past that. She-She did neither; fuckin' hair always nappy, she bathed probably once a week, and she acted like the world owed her something. I couldn't fuck with nobody like that, not even to get my dick sucked," he mumbled that last part more to himself.

"I thought y'all said she was married," I interrupted.

"SHE IS," they both spoke unanimously. "Rohan was locked up for years, he ain't got no money for no divorce lawyer."

"So where she get a baby from?"

"Creeping out here to visit her sister in Chicago," Vahan continued. "Her and her sister out here snorting that shit and ran out of money. I was at my girl crib, so they ran across Hamm thirsty ass. Nigga told them he'd give them a half if they both let him hit."

"Oooooh, THAT'S how Hamm knocked off Eisha's ol' girl," I chuckled before taking a puff from my cigar and sipping from the shot of cognac sitting in front of me.

"Yup. He actually knocked both of them off that night; they kids was about to be sister-cousins or whatever you call 'em. Soon as She-She realized what she did and remembered her vows, she tried going back to the old country and telling everybody that she hit a lick in the states and was about to be that deal. According to her, she had me gone off the pussy. Meanwhile, she went and had a conjugal visit with her husband so he didn't suspect nothing. Word got back to Virginie, next thing I know her and Philomené pull up. On a jet, mind you. Virginie got off that plane and beat the shit out of She-She, she lost that baby. I ain't never crossed that woman again after that. Gave her everything she wanted, even some shit she didn't," Vahan finished, his eyes twinkling. I got a feeling it was more than just her kicking Free's mama's ass that got her whatever she wanted though.

"That's when she started hatching a plan to get on Team Hermes, talking bout I raped Siranush—" Pop began.

"Pop, you took some pussy from somebody?"

"HELL NAW. I gave Free's mother the money to get her husband out of jail, so you wouldn't have to marry her. Already made arrangements with the judge and everything; all she had to do was go give the man the money. It couldn't come from me for obvious reasons. Found out after the fact that She-She kept the money, said it was for the pain and suffering that she'd gone through for the years Rohan was locked up. I wanted to talk to Free and explain that I made a mistake; I couldn't force you to be with her if you didn't want to. She came outside with no bra on and tried coming on to me. I told her no, and when my security team heard that, they came around the corner. Next thing I knew, she was butt naked and—"

"Getting down how she lived," I finished for him as me and Unc laughed while dapping each other up.

"So when I finally got a chance to talk to her, the bitch said I raped her. Fucked up part was that She-She watched the whole thing from the kitchen window. They already had the plan together before we got the officiant out there the next day, and I didn't want to look like an asshole with the whole village there knowing Free was supposed to marry Atif. Y'all right, I do need to sit this one out because although I know she fucked up, I still think she's a broken girl with no real guidance trying to make it in this world."

"You know him and ya mama back fucking, right?" Vahan turned to me and smiled crazily. "That's why he all soft an' shit, acting all goofy all of a sudden."

"I ain't wanna know that, Unc."

"You had a hand in this too, Atif. Getting some good pussy from his girl and you gave him grandkids. Aram, they call you Grandad or Pee-Paw? You tuck them in and read bedtime stories too?" Vahan teased.

"Fuck you, Vahan." Pop pushed his chair back from the table and walked over to pour himself a second shot of Louis XIII. "Wait til' Tanji drop that load, your grandkids gonna call you Grandad too," I heard him mumble as he walked past.

"What's up with my daughter-in-law, Atif? This Free thing the only thing she got going on?"

"Nah, she got beef with her ex-husband's current hoe. I'll handle that, though."

"You sure? You know I'll clear out a block quick."

"Unc, I got this."

"A'ight. Call me if you need something though."

"I got your number, Unc."

"Then use it. Make sure Tanji use it too."

"I will."

---

FOR ALL THEIR DIFFERENCES, it was crazy how much Free and Kapri were alike. Free's mother was just as manipulative as Kapri's; had she came and just talked to me instead of killing my brother, I might've been able to help her out too.

Checking my phone, I saw she responded to my text to meet up out in Oak Park later on that night. I told her we needed to come up with some sort of resolution to our issues, because we couldn't keep going back and forth. People were dying, and I didn't want her to harm anyone else in my family. She fell for all that soft nigga bullshit.

I politicked with the O.G.'s for a little while longer, then headed out. Traffic was light this time of night, so it only took me about twenty minutes to go from the city to the suburbs. I pulled into the Walgreens parking lot on Madison and waited until I saw the black Bentley with Wisconsin plates pull up and park in front of me. Free got out dressed in a tight-fitting dress with black heels; she would've been slightly sexy if she wasn't shaped like a box.

"Hey Atif," she purred once she got in my trap truck. "I knew you'd come back to me."

"I just think this is all a big misunderstanding," I spoke, pulling out of the parking lot. "People don't need to keep dying because of our situation."

"That's true," she smiled, looking like a gorilla. "Have you thought about my proposal?"

"I have, and I think it's actually a good idea," I agreed, glancing in the rear view mirror as we sat at the stop light. Unc's people blinked their headlights at me subtly; I turned to her with a smile as the light turned green. "I already put in a few calls to the old country to get us a whole new team. Real gangsters for this Armenian mob."

"I can't believe I'm going to be the head of a crime family in the United States!" she gushed. "Mama will be so proud!"

"Yea, we gotta figure out what state we gonna have the house built; here or Wisconsin," I continued, merging onto the Eisenhower expressway.

"What about Kapri?"

"I told her that I want my real wife back. She was mad, but she'll get over it."

"What about the baby?"

"She giving me my baby girl," I lied. "We not even gonna co-parent, she giving me full custody. You ready to be a mother?"

"Oh, Atif yes! YES! That's all I ever wanted from you," she reached over to stroke my face lovingly.

"Remember our wedding night, Siran?"

"Of course. How can I forget?"

"You was trying to tell me something when the guards put you out the house. Talk to me, baby," I mumbled, running my finger down her cheek.

"Your father had some men come to my house to rape me," she whispered, closing her eyes and leaning in to my touch. "I couldn't believe he'd do that to me."

"Pop had some men come rape you? Why would he do that?"

"I don't know."

"Come on now, Siranush. You gotta tell me the truth, our relationship can't be built on no lies."

"They didn't rape me," she admitted, licking my fingers. "My mother made me take off my underwear before I went outside and told me to rub against your father. She said I could get more money for being with both of you; I could be with your father while you were here and vice versa. Your father didn't know what was going on, and since his security team was there, I figured the impact would be the same. She told me to say those things so she could extort more money from your father."

"Y'all family ain't that fucked up financially that she need to be moving like that, though," I mumbled lowly. "She be making them heatmakers for every muthafuckin' body."

"I can't speak for her, Atif, I can only tell you what I know to be true."

"But why though?"

"I've been doing things for my family ever since I was a little girl. My father didn't know, but my mother did. She wanted our family name to be synonymous with the Hermes dynasty back home."

Rubbing my beard, it hit me that I was a God for real, not just a muthafucka that people feared and respected based off of how I moved out here. Bitches out here setting they own damn kids up just to be on my level. That was fucked up, but it wasn't my life nor my business. Like I said before, had we had this conversation before we said 'I do', Free would be on her way to living her best life instead of me about to end her shit. "Aye, we need to be celebrating our reunion." I glanced at her briefly, shooting her a sly smile. "You wanna give your husband some pussy?" I cleared my throat to keep from choking on my own words.

"You not gonna put another pillowcase over my head, are you?" she asked seriously. I had to turn my head to stop the memory of that heinous night.

"Nah, baby. I wanna look you in your eyes while you give me that good stuff." If she knew me as well as a wife should know her husband, she'd know I was lying. I didn't even talk like that.

"Yes Atif! I'd love to give you some!" she cheered.

"Aye, you know what I like?"

"What?"

"Getting my dick sucked. Man, I'ma fuck the shit outta you if you suck it while we driving to the spot."

"We going to your house in Kenilworth?"

"Mmhmm."

She unzipped my pants and wrapped her dry lips on my shit. I thought her tongue would cut my dick; it felt like sandpaper.

"You like that, Atif?"

I grabbed a sucker from the armrest, unwrapping it and passed it to her. "Here. Suck on this for a few minutes, then try it again."

"What's a sucker supposed to do?"

"It's gonna help make your mouth feel like a warm, wet pussy. Curl your tongue around it and let the juices run down your throat, a'ight?"

"Atif, I don't understand..."

"That's how these American women do it. For me, baby?" I stroked her cheek and spoke gently.

She deep throated the candy, pushing it in and pulling it out of her lips trying to look sexy for me. Switching my thoughts to my girl, I missed feeling her mouth on me, twirling her tongue around the tip and sucking my balls. *Damn, Kapri.* Leaning my head back, I couldn't help but to smirk when I heard her bite the candy, the crunching noises filling the truck's space before she swallowed loudly.

"That was a little too sweet...Atif, I feel...I feel funny. Why is the car so hot? I can't catch my...." she began wheezing loudly.

"Oh, oops. That must be one of those Fentanyl lollipops I got from Unc," I cackled watching as her eyes widened and her hand went up to her throat. "My bad."

"Whyyyy...." she begged with her eyes bucked as her breathing slowed.

"You don't fuck with a man's family," I spoke gently, pulling over on the bridge. "You especially don't threaten the God."

Watching her pupils dilate as she stopped breathing, I rubbed my hands together like Baby seeing Unc's people pull up behind me, opening the door and yanking her body out of the passenger seat. "We'll take it from here, God."

"Good looking," I responded, watching as they pulled concrete cinder blocks, ropes and sheets from the trunk of their car. "Maybe not Mrs. Al Capone, more like Mrs. Jimmy Hoffa," I snarled watching as they quickly wrapped her up in sheets, securing the cinder blocks to her ankles before tossing her body over the Chicago River bridge.

---

SECOND ON MY list was this Tangelica chick causing lil' sis stress. I tried to let her handle it, but the more I thought about it, the more I needed to make sure she relaxed. She was still in the early stages of her pregnancy, according to Ma she was still touch and go. With her still mourning lil' bro's death, I had to make sure everything else was smooth for her.

"Whaddup AZ," I hit up my lawyer/partner in the streets. "You take care of that business for me?"

"Just sent it to your phone, G," he yawned. "What time is it?"

"Man...streets just now coming alive and yo' ass in the bed like an old man," I chuckled, glancing at the console which read 3:09 a.m.

"God, you know I got court in the morning. These judges try and get over on you if you ain't operating at one hundred twenty percent when you walk through those doors," he yawned a second time.

"A'ight my G. Call me tomorrow."

"No doubt," he mumbled before hanging up.

I checked the text message that AZ sent and turned my truck to the Four Seasons, which was a few blocks from where I was. Passing the valet the keys to my trap truck, I pulled the Bulls fitted down over my eyes and headed up the fire steps. This bitch was on the third floor, so I didn't have to go too far. Tapping three times on the door to her suite, I turned my back to the cameras and waited.

"Who is it?" a muffled voice finally called out sleepily.

"Aye baby, it's me."

"Me who?"

"Leon."

I heard the latch move from the door jamb as she unlocked the dead bolt.

"Leon baby I thought...wait...you ain't Leon." She stood confused as I pushed her forcefully inside the suite.

"How can you say that about your man?" I grumbled with my hand around her neck. "Much pussy as you done gave up, now you don't know me? Where my babies at?"

"I..." she gasped for air, trying to scratch up my arm to get some DNA under her nails. Too bad I had a nice coat of Vaseline on my hands and arms for occasions like these. "...you killed Steve," she breathed.

"Fuck Steve."

"How..." I watched her eyes as she struggled to catch her breath, her hands slipping each time she reached for me.

"Leon? DNA, boo. And we got access to hospital cameras. Imagine my surprise seeing this nigga Leon hugging and kissing that little boy that you insist is Steve's? You shoulda just left Tanji's ass alone," I growled, feeling something snap before her breath halted in her throat. Her eyes were permanently frozen in fright as I picked her dead body up and laid her gently on the bed, covering her up before leaving her suite. Sending AZ a text to have the hotel's security cameras wiped from 3:10 a.m. to 4:14 a.m., I tossed the valet a couple of hundreds for his silence and headed to the west side. I had one more stop before I could hop a plane to the A.

"POP, what you doing out here, my G?" I dapped him up after I parked my trap truck next to his rental car sitting on the next block.

"AZ called and told me about this Monica person." He gave me a quick man hug. "I knew you was taking care of Free, and he called me about an hour ago saying you had the cameras at some chick's hotel wiped. I knew you'd be headed this way next."

"Yeah, this bird talking bout she pregnant by me. All this time I been nutting on this bitch back and she been good, now since I stop fucking her she pregnant."

"Atif, you already know how that go," he cackled, dapping me up again. Pop was petty as hell when he wanted to be. "Just another one of the Hermes curses."

"What? Good dick?"

"Yup. You see how your mama..."

"POP! I don't wanna hear that shit!" I yelled as he laughed. "You been in there yet?" I motioned towards Steve's mother's home.

"Yeah. Ooooo...Steve mama a hoe!" he chuckled.

"What she do?"

"Just know I ain't cheat on my baby." He tugged on his waistband a few times with a guilty smirk on his face. "That Monica ain't gonna bother you no more, son."

"Is she still alive?"

"Yeah. She still breathing."

"Pop. What did you do?"

"Nothing," he insisted innocently. "We just had a friendly conversation."

"About?"

"Something she thought nobody knew about that I do."

"How you know, Pop?"

"Come on, son. I'm tired as hell, let's ride down to Atlanta. I miss my baby." He patted me on the back and we walked to our vehicles together.

"Where's Unc?"

"He left after his people called to tell him about Siranush. Said something about setting up some meetings with some contractors and real estate agents before he went back home."

I tried texting Monica since Pop was being so secretive, but I got an error message back that my text hadn't gone through. Pulling out my trap phone, I called her number and she answered.

"Hel...hello?" she whispered, sounding like she was sneaking on the phone.

"Monica?"

"God?"

"Aye..."

"Don't call me no more! Please leave me alone!" she screamed before hanging up.

*Fuck it,* I thought to myself, staring briefly at the phone before tucking it back in my pocket. *Bitch crazy anyway.* I headed to the airport with Pop; Ma said the flight was only two hours. When I finally laid down to rest, it would be next to my lady and my baby. Atlanta was an hour ahead, so I hoped somebody had some shrimp and grits done by the time I got there.

# THIRTY-THREE

## KAPRI

### FIVE MONTHS LATER

"ATIIIIFF!"

"What's wrong, baby?" He rolled over sleepily, his hand automatically reaching for my belly. "Eww, you peed in the bed?"

"My water broke, boy!" I punched him in the arm. "Remember earlier when I told you I felt funny and you told me to just get on top?"

"Damn girl, you in labor?" he rubbed his eyes sleepily. "Tell Junior I need thirty more minutes."

"Junior ain't waiting on you, Mr. Hermes." I snatched the pillow from underneath his head and raised it over my head to smack him again until that contraction knocked me on my ass.

"AAAHHH!"

"KAPRI, WHAT'S WRONG!"

"Did you hear me? I'M IN LABOR!" I screamed.

"Oh, shit, I thought I was dreaming!" He hopped up and ran to the closet to grab my hospital bag. Running back to the bed where I sat watching him, he quickly tossed the bag over his shoulder and reached down to pick me up from our king-sized bed.

"Baby, you forgetting something," I murmured in his ear, wrapping my arms around his neck.

"What? I got you, spare keys in the side pocket, you got a couple of dollars, right?"

"Put some clothes on, love. Your dick is out," I snickered.

He put me back on the bed, laughing with me. "That pussy was good last night, too."

"It's good every night, what you talking about?" I giggled. "Come on now, your son is just as overbearing...AAAHHH!"

"How far apart are your contractions?"

"About five minutes," I breathed through it. They were coming stronger and longer. "Come on Atif before I have this baby in the back seat of the Wraith!"

Atif rushed out the closet with his basketball shorts on backwards and his t-shirt inside out. Picking me back up, I wrapped my arms around his neck for a second time as he ran and tapped on the door to his mother's room. "MA! WE BOUT TO GO!"

"Here I come, baby," she called out. We heard a lot of bumping and it sounded like somebody tripped when Papa Hermes pulled the door open.

"We'll be up there later, son. Call us," he smiled happily.

"Y'all need to stop fucking in my house," Atif leaned over and mumbled in his father's ear. "My kids here and y'all loud."

"We just christening the new place," Papa Hermes replied. These two made me wonder who was the father and who was the son.

"ATIIIFF!"

"Bye Pop," he waved his father off and we ran out the house as quickly as possible. Our son was coming whether his grandparents were getting their freak on under our roof or not. I was glad Atif's mother came to stay with us during the last few months of my pregnancy; she made some of the best seafood gumbo on the planet.

Pulling up the hospital's address on the GPS, the quickest way with the least traffic at that time of night was taking the causeway. Since we moved to Miami a few months ago, Atif and I loved riding the causeway at night watching the twinkling lights from the city dancing on the water.

"Kapri, thank you."

"What I do now? AAAHHH!"

"Breathe like the doctors taught you, love," he coached, reaching in the back seat to rub my belly. "Your stomach hard. Wait, where did the baby go?"

"Atif, I think..."

"What?"

"Oh, God! I think he's coming now!" I screamed. "PULL OVER!"

Luckily we hadn't hit the causeway yet, Atif hit a traffic light that he was trying to run and I stopped him. We swerved off the road and onto the beach; Atif turned the car off and hurried to open the back door where I had my legs gaped apart trying not to push.

"Kapri..."

"CALL THE AMBULANCE!" I yelled. "I'M ABOUT TO PUSH, ATIF CALL THE AMBULANCE!" I cried.

As he patted his pockets to find his phone, a couple came over to check on me and make sure I was okay.

"Sir, I'm a doctor. Is there anything I can do?" I heard a voice call out over the crashing waves.

"I think I saw my son's head," I heard Atif say to the nice couple as the breeze blowing off of the ocean cooled me down some, but not much.

"Okay, if that's the case, we need to get him out quickly," the man spoke professionally, springing into action. "Honey, pass me the cooler," he spoke to the woman.

"Hol' on, what y'all got in that cooler?" Atif questioned suspiciously.

"Ice and some bottled water," the woman put his mind at ease. "And a bottle of Dom Perignon. We had a late night picnic," the woman soothed. "Sorry, the cheese and crackers are gone."

"Okay, just making sure," I heard the edge leave Atif's voice slightly. "I don't wanna have to snap y'all necks or nothing out here," he chuckled nervously as the woman suddenly shot him a leery glare. Her movements told me she was just a little scared.

"ATIIIIFFF!"

"Lift your bottom up a little, miss," the older white man directed gently as he slid a blanket underneath me. "Your son is crowning; a few pushes and he'll be out. I need you to calm down and breathe, okay?"

Nodding my head as the ambulance sirens screamed in the distance, I took two deep breaths as the contractions turned into one long pain in my pelvis. Everything below my waistline was killing me. "Okay."

"I'm going to count to three, and you give me one big push. One...two...th..."

I started pushing before he could get the full number out; all those videos I watched where the women swore a natural birth was best told a damn lie. Junior was trying to stand up and walk out of my uterus.

"You're doing good, Kapri," Atif coached from behind the doctor as he recorded our son's entrance into the world. "Give me one more big push, baby."

The blinking red and blue lights from behind him were irritating the hell out of me as I felt the worst pain I've ever felt in my life. It wasn't coming from the baby; my head suddenly began to pound so hard I saw a heartbeat behind my pupils. I had to get Junior out though.

"Okay, one more..." the older white man's voice sounded far away as a ringing noise overtook my hearing. "One...two..." I felt Junior being pulled from my body as Atif yelled in the background.

"Kapri, he's here! Look at...Kapri? KAPRIIIIII!"

# THIRTY-FOUR

## ATIF

"I'll get the baby, son," Mama spoke quietly from behind me. Junior was a good baby, he hardly ever cried unless he was hungry or needed to be changed. Other than that, he wasn't spoiled or nothing, considering how much everyone held him after the funeral.

Standing inside the closet running my hand over her things, I couldn't believe she was gone. We were supposed to raise our children together; it wasn't supposed to be this. Kapri was the most self-less woman I'd ever known. She cared too much about everyone else but herself. The doctors said she had a blood clot in her brain that came out of nowhere. The lights from the ambulance caused her brain to have a mini seizure, causing the clot to travel quicker and that's what she...

"FUCK!"

"Is there anything I can do for you, son?" Pop came in my room and kneeled in front of me as I sat on the bed with my head in my hands.

"Bring her back to me, Pop. That's all I need, just give her back to me."

"Atif, if I could..."

"I'm good, then."

"Son, if you need to talk, I'm here."

"I know. Thanks, man." I stood up and walked out on the balcony to watch the afternoon waves. Kapri loved this house, man. She picked it out back while we were still in the city; this was the house we were supposed to come see that day. This was the house we were supposed to raise our kids in, this was the house we were supposed to grow old together in. This was our family home. How was it a home when she wasn't here in it?

No woman ever brought me to tears but smelling her scent on her pillow every night had me breaking down; I hadn't slept in days. I saw how Tanji felt when she lost Prince. Unc had her come back to Armenia with him and Prince's mother. That wasn't an option for me. Not anymore.

My mind wandered back to that night on the beach when my wife gave birth to my son and I lost her, both in the same breath. I didn't believe in karma and all that other nonsense. If you asked me what my sign was, I'd cuss your ass out. As the paramedics rushed to clean my son up and check out his vitals while working to find a pulse on my wife, I backed up and realized the beach we were standing on was the same one where I met my son for the first time when I was in that coma.

*"Kapri, don't leave me. DON'T LEAVE ME!" I yelled as the doctor who delivered my son pronounced her dead.*

"Hey, Atif, how you holdin' up big bro?" Jacari asked barging into my room without knocking with Jacoby behind him.

"Aye, I'm coping, lil bro. Y'all good?" I wiped the tear from my cheek before turning to face them both.

"It's hard," Jacoby admitted. "Kapri was like a mother to us. She made sure that we always had what we needed, even when our mother didn't." *Do I tell him now? Nah. If he hates me when he gets older for keeping this from him, then that's what it is.*

"I know, 'Coby. Your sister was one of the good ones."

"I'm gonna miss her, 'Tif. I love my sister," he sniffed.

"Me too, lil' bro. Me too. But she'll always be with us."

"Us? Wait, you not making us go back to Chicago?" Jacoby frowned.

"Going back to Chicago? With who?"

"I thought you kept us around because..."

"Look," I pulled them both back in the house and sat them down on the edge of my bed. "Y'all my brothers. I told y'all that the day I took y'all to Prince mama house. That means y'all MY responsibility. Not Kapri's, not Prince mama, hell not y'all mama. My love for y'all is in addition to the love I have for y'all sister. Just because she gone don't mean that stops."

"Told you he wasn't gonna send us back to the people," Jacoby spoke smugly.

"What people? Aye, who told y'all I was sending y'all anywhere?"

"Jacari." 'Coby pointed at his brother. "He said you was gonna send us back to Chicago with the social worker lady."

"I just thought..." Jacari began.

"Fuck that social worker lady. Y'all my brothers and that's it, a'ight?"

"A'ight," they both dapped me up before heading back to their bedrooms. "I'ma have people start calling me God too." I heard Jacari yell down the hallway before hearing the door to his bedroom slam.

*Kapri, we don't need another me around here.* I talked to my wife as I sometimes did when I was alone. *Talk to your brother.*

*I will.*

Sometimes...in my mind...she answered me.

**The End**

# ABOUT THE AUTHOR

Thanks for reading! If you enjoyed the series, please leave me a review on Amazon or my Facebook page! I love hearing from my readers, you guys are the BEST!

Have you joined my mailing list? Click here: www.fatimasbooks.com
Love Fatima Munroe? Join my street team! Start here:
http://bit.ly/TeamFatima
Did you LOVE Vega and Domenica's story? Get caught up:
http://bit.ly/1LoveU2

Follow me on social media!
Facebook: http://facebook.com/authorfatimamunroe
Twitter: http://twitter.com/fatimamunroe
IG: http://instagram.com/fatima_munroe
Be on the lookout for my next series coming this summer!

COMING 07/23!

CPSIA information can be obtained
at www.ICGtesting.com
Printed in the USA
LVHW031455050619
620258LV00014B/843/P